LOCKSMITH

LOCKSMITH

Nicholas Maes

DUNDURN PRESS
TORONTO

Editor: Michael Carroll
Designer: Courtney Horner
Printer: Webcom

Library and Archives Canada Cataloguing in Publication

Maes, Nicholas, 1960-
     Locksmith / Nicholas Maes.

ISBN 978-1-55002-791-4

     I. Title.

PS8626.A37L63 2008   jC813'.6   C2008-900681-X

1   2   3   4   5   12   11   10   09   08

Conseil des Arts
du Canada

Canada Council
for the Arts

Canada

ONTARIO ARTS COUNCIL
CONSEIL DES ARTS DE L'ONTARIO

We acknowledge the support of the **Canada Council for the Arts** and the **Ontario Arts Council** for our publishing program. We also acknowledge the financial support of the **Government of Canada** through the **Book Publishing Industry Development Program** and **The Association for the Export of Canadian Books**, and the **Government of Ontario** through the **Ontario Book Publishers Tax Credit program** and the **Ontario Media Development Corporation**.

Care has been taken to trace the ownership of copyright material used in this book. The author and the publisher welcome any information enabling them to rectify any references or credits in subsequent editions.

J. Kirk Howard, President

Printed and bound in Canada
www.dundurn.com

Dundurn Press	Gazelle Book Services Limited	Dundurn Press
3 Church Street, Suite 500	White Cross Mills	2250 Military Road
Toronto, Ontario, Canada	High Town, Lancaster, England	Tonawanda, NY
M5E 1M2	LA1 4XS	U.S.A. 14150

To Gershom, Yehuda, and Miriam: what father has ever been blessed with such riches?

Acknowledgements

Heartfelt thanks to my wife, Deborah, who read *Locksmith* with the eye of an appreciative child (and not a scoffing critic), and thanks also to my editor, Michael Carroll, who has a soft spot for stories about maniacal chemists and made this book possible.

CHAPTER

Lewis Castorman was way behind schedule. His alarm clock had gone off at half-past seven, but he had stayed in bed and had waited for his father to wake him. It was only at 7:56 a.m. when the radio played an ad for the Fort Knox Locking System that his dark brown eyes opened in worry and he remembered that his father hadn't come home.

Today was what? Lewis glanced at a calendar from Houdini Armour and Company and saw that it was Tuesday already. His dad should have been home the Friday before. Saturday would have been okay, but Sunday was ... preposterous! His father had been late before, like that time he had opened a swing bridge in Florida, but he had always telephoned to keep Lewis informed. So why this silence for five long days?

"Lewis!"

At the sound of Mrs. Gibson's voice Lewis ran for his clothes.

"Hurry up! We overslept and you'll be late for school!"

"I'll be down in a minute, Mrs. Gibson," Lewis called, stuffing a leather case into his pocket after checking to see that all its picks were inside. "Always have your tools on hand," his father continually told him. "Because you never know when a door will lock behind you." His equipment in place, Lewis entered the bathroom, where he washed his face and combed his chestnut hair. He stared at his reflection.

"Dad's okay," he whispered to himself. "It's not like ... you know what. He'll be home in time for supper."

"I've prepared some oatmeal," Mrs. Gibson announced when Lewis was seated at the kitchen table. "I had to make it quickly because I slept through my alarm."

"It smells delicious," Lewis said, wondering why there was onion peel in it.

"And be sure to drink up," Mrs. Gibson added, handing him a glass of juice that smelled like cheese.

"Thanks," Lewis said, containing a groan. Mrs. Gibson had been with them for almost a year, but he still wasn't used to her cooking habits — the way she mixed weird ingredients together, then expressed surprise when he didn't want to eat.

And her cooking was just the tip of the iceberg. He had seen her every day for the past twelve months, but her appearance still struck him as unusual. Not only was she large —six foot six and four hundred pounds — but her head was wide and football-shaped, and beneath a mask of talcum powder her skin was green. Her hair was orange, thick as cord, and looked a lot like an old floor mop. She also wore a pair of rubber gloves and a metal ring around her neck — for good luck, she explained. Finally, her voice was lower than his father's, and he had seen her eat six apple pies in one sitting.

"Good morning, everyone," Mr. Todrey announced,

emerging from the back room and sitting at the table. "Aren't you two running behind schedule?"

Mrs. Gibson sniffed. "I got up late. Although it's hardly your concern."

"Is there any oatmeal left?" he asked, scanning the front page of the *Mason Springs Gazette*, "New York State's Finest Morning Paper." "It smells delicious."

"There is, but I'm eating it. I'm Lewis's housekeeper, not your personal cook."

"Look at that," Mr. Todrey said. "Grumpel's closing branches in Maine and Quebec. He's shut eight factories over the past three months."

"Don't mention his name!" the housekeeper cried.

"But it's odd," he mused. "Everyone's nuts about his chemicals, so why are his companies shrinking in number? If anything, he should be opening new branches."

"I said don't mention his name in this kitchen!"

"All right. Calm down. There's an article here about Yellow Swamp. I'll read it in silence if you'll serve me some oatmeal …"

Mr. Todrey might have been Mrs. Gibson's twin. Not only was he the exact same size, but his skin betrayed an identical shade of green under a lavish coating of Grumpel's Facial Ointment. His orange moustache was just like her hair, and he wore rubber gloves and a ring around his neck. Needless to say, this was more than a coincidence.

Unlike Mrs. Gibson, however, Mr. Todrey liked chemistry textbooks. When he wasn't reading the paper, or filching snacks from the kitchen, he was wrapping his head around molecular acids, ionized suspensions, and nucleonic squeezes.

But he was nervous, Mr. Todrey was. The man was always peering out the window and asking Lewis about the people he had seen. If Lewis mentioned he had talked to a stranger, or that his class had been taught by a substitute teacher, Mr. Todrey would gasp and question him closely. Who were these people? Had they asked where Lewis lived? Had they mentioned anyone named Gibiwink or Todrus?

Lewis sometimes suspected Mr. Todrey had broken some law, but his father always laughed at this suggestion and said they were lucky to have such interesting tenants.

His father. Lewis's fears flooded back with a vengeance. Why wasn't he home? Why hadn't he phoned? Had he met with trouble? Had there been an accident? To stop himself from panicking, Lewis left the table. "I'm off," he declared.

"You haven't eaten anything," Mrs. Gibson wailed.

"I'll be late," Lewis called, moving toward the door.

"What about your homework?" Mr. Todrey asked.

"My composition!" Lewis cried. "Thanks. I almost forgot."

He approached a staircase that led to the basement. At the head of these stairs stood a squat wooden column whose top had been fitted with a strip of glass. The glass was blue and was tilted at a sixty-degree angle. Holding his hand to the glass, Lewis smiled as a sensor scanned his handprint and caused a bolt on the downstairs door to open, at which stage several lights in the stairwell flickered on. He descended the steps two at a time. By the time he reached the bottom, the basement door had opened and the well-lit space beyond was visible. As he crossed the threshold, he felt his worries lift.

From outside, the house appeared ordinary. Modest in size and a little rough around the edges, with its peeling paint and weed-choked lawn, it wasn't anything special to look at. And the interior was the same, with its worn furniture, books, and simple knickknacks. Normal people whose idea of an exciting time was to watch the late-night movie on television — that was what these furnishings said.

The basement suggested a very different picture. It was cluttered with materials to the point of bursting. There were tools of every size, shape, and colour: drills, table saws, lathes, and metal presses. Blocks of steel were piled in one corner, and beside them was a selection of cogs of every conceivable size and design. And then there were the interesting gadgets — infrared sensors, high-grade lasers, and coils tipped with miniature cameras, ones you could steer inside the larger locking mechanisms.

Lewis approached a table that ran the length of the basement and thought about the hours he had spent in this room. From an early age his parents had brought him into this space and patiently taught him every trick of the trade, every known way to construct a lock and get it open.

Locks. They were scattered across the table. Some were very run-of-the-mill — the padlock, combination lock, surface auxiliary and pin tumbler cylinders. Then there were the others: the titanium "gridiron" for high-security prisons, the convex "strangulator" for an F-18 fighter plane, the phantom hyperlink that was said to be unbreakable …

Unbreakable. Lewis recalled an exchange between his parents a month before the disaster had struck and two days after his eleventh birthday.

"There's no such thing as unbreakable," his father had joked.

"I disagree," his mother had said. "One day I'll build a lock that even you can't open."

"Like the Blackhawk 33?" his father had teased.

"The modulator was faulty! And the clamping system almost had you fooled!"

"But I did pick it in the end."

"I'm telling you, I'll build an unbreakable lock. You'll see!"

He closed his eyes. It would never happen. He remembered waiting for his mother to show. For days on end he had sat by the phone, hanging on her call. Then his father had walked into the kitchen one night — that was the very same day their tenants had moved in — and with a look of devastation had told him the bad news.

His father. Where was he? Why hadn't he phoned? Was history repeating itself?

"Stop it!" he whispered. "Get a grip on yourself!"

His composition was lying at the end of the table. He picked it up, crammed it in his knapsack, and turned toward the basement exit. As he climbed the stairs, the heavy door locked behind him and sensors dimmed the lights one by one.

"What about your lunch?" Mrs. Gibson asked as he emerged on the ground floor and hurried to the door.

"No time!" Lewis cried, scrambling outside. "I'll see you later!"

"But it's your favourite!" Mrs. Gibson yelled, holding up a bologna sandwich with mould on its crusts.

Quick as a flash, Mr. Todrey gulped the sandwich down. "No point letting it go to waste," he said, beaming.

Lewis heard the housekeeper scream from halfway down the block.

CHAPTER 2

With the early-morning sunlight on his shoulders, Lewis ran to 30 Grumpel Lane. It was a house that might have been confused with his except that its roof was freshly tiled, its walls were painted an elegant green, the lawn was trimmed, and there were flowers everywhere. From a window on the ground floor there came the smell of breakfast — waffles with blueberries and maple syrup. There was also the sound of angry voices. As usual they were arguing.

"Don't lie! You ate all the waffles you pig!"

"Can you prove it?"

"Don't get smart! Just because you're puny doesn't mean —"

"That's not proof. You're insulting me."

"Alfonse!" Lewis called out, hating to intrude when Alfonse was fighting with his sister. "We've got to go. We're going to be late."

"Hi, Lewis. Sure. I'll be there in a moment."

"Move those comics from the table first! You know why you read this junk? To make up for your skinny dimensions!"

"Better that than playing the piano off-key."

"Alfonse!" Lewis insisted. "We have to hurry."

A moment later Alfonse came running out, a bundle in his right hand and a knapsack on his shoulders. As usual he looked eight and not his real age of eleven. He tried to exaggerate his size by dressing as an adult — he was wearing a tie and an old tweed jacket — but if anything this clothing made him seem even scrawnier.

"Adelaide's angry?" Lewis asked as they set off down the road.

"She thinks I ate her waffles. Little does she know."

"You don't have to feed me," Lewis protested as Alfonse handed him a sticky bundle. Peeling back a napkin, he found four waffles inside.

"What was it this time?" Alfonse asked, "Oatmeal with onion or pancakes with olives?"

"Oatmeal. Still, you shouldn't make Adelaide angry …"

"I'm only acting in self-defence."

Lewis nodded and bit into his breakfast. For as long as he and Alfonse had been pals, he had never heard him exchange a kind word with his sister. Maybe they were too close in age — Adelaide was ten months older than her brother. Or perhaps they fought because they never saw their parents. The family bakery was an expensive business — their landlord Mr. Grumpel charged a fortune in rent — and the Pangettis had to work like slaves to pay their monthly bills.

"Never mind her," Alfonse said, shrugging as they crossed a vacant lot that led to Grumpel Corner. "You should read the latest issue of *The Bombardier*. Dr. Camphor invents a chemical that he slips into people's food. With it he can hypnotize —"

"My father's still not home," Lewis interjected.

"Has he phoned?"

"No. And it's been five days."

"Should I tell my parents? We can stop off at the bakery."

"I'll wait one more day. If he's not home tomorrow, I'll call the police."

"He must be busy with a lock or something."

"Maybe," Lewis conceded. "But I wish he'd call."

Both of them gasped. They had turned from Grumpel Corner onto Grumpel Way and now saw a block ahead of them that a crowd had gathered in front of Grumpel's Bank. Police and firemen had arrived on the scene and were trying to control the situation. Although the boys were late for school already, they were dying to know what this fuss was about.

The spectators on the outer ring were talking among themselves — how time was running out and it was a horrible way to go. A little farther in five policemen held people back and muttered that the guy was as good as doomed. Sneaking past these guards, the boys overheard a knot of firemen say that their efforts were a waste of time. Finally, at the very heart of the crowd a television crew was idling about, and their leader, a bone-thin woman in black, kept shoving a microphone in people's faces and asking stupid questions.

The boys glanced at each other. What the heck was going on?

A big man in a uniform drew near, his bull-like features drawn tight with concern. Behind him was the woman from the television station. He was about to issue orders, but she thrust herself in front of him, within hearing distance of Lewis and Alfonse.

"Fire Marshal Stephens!" she cried. "Can you tell us how this crisis is unfolding?"

"You know the facts," the big fellow growled. "A man's trapped inside the bank vault. The lock's on a timer and can't be opened for hours, but in the next ten minutes his air will run out."

"You can't force the vault open?" the woman asked.

"We'd have to use explosives, and the chances are the guy would get killed. But if we don't act soon, his oxygen will —"

"There's the guy's family!" a cameraman yelled. Immediately, the reporter abandoned the fire marshal and hurried to a woman whose face was twitching. Beside her was a three-year-old boy who was smiling because of people's attention, too young to understand that his father was in danger. Even as the television crew swarmed this lady, Stephens glanced at his watch. With a sigh he told his men to unload three crates off a truck. Each crate bore the words DANGER: HIGH EXPLOSIVES.

"Too bad The Bombardier isn't here," Alfonse whispered. "He'd melt the door with his gamma-ray vision."

"Excuse me, sir," Lewis said, approaching the fire marshal.

"Pile 'em against the vault!" Stephens shouted. "We'll blow the door and hope for the best."

"Please, Mr. Stephens," Lewis persisted, plucking the officer's gold-braided sleeve. "I was wondering —"

"And move this crowd back!" the marshal ordered.

"Just in case the blast's too strong!"

"Listen!" Lewis demanded, blocking the head fireman's path. "I need some information about the vault. Can you tell me its model and serial number?"

"Faster!" the marshal cried. "We've got eight minutes. As for you, son, get out of the way. A life's at stake and I haven't —"

"What's the model?" Lewis repeated. "Is it an XPJ or a High-Fusion Special?"

"Huh?" the marshal snorted in confusion.

"Please. What model are you dealing with?"

"It's an XPJ, the 2000 series ..."

"In that case," Lewis declared, "I'll need a paper clip, wire, and a stick of chewing gum."

"Chewing gum?" Stephens bellowed. "Look, kid, this is a serious business!"

"This is Lewis Castorman," Alfonse piped up. "He's an experienced locksmith."

"And my mother designed the XPJ," Lewis explained. "Please, sir, I can open that vault."

Stephens studied Lewis closely. At that moment two firemen passed with a crate whose sides bore a skull and crossbones. The sight of the TNT made the marshal grimace. "Sam! Will!" he called to his men. "Drop the crate and find me a paper clip, wire, and ... and ..."

"A stick of chewing gum," Lewis added.

Muttering to himself that he must be crazy, Stephens escorted the boys into the bank, brushing aside the reporter in black who was lurking like a wolf beside the front entrance. At the back of the bank, behind a long marble counter, a heavy door with metal bars stood open. Two clerks were guarding it and talking to each other. One was betting fifty bucks that the guy would die of oxygen starvation, while his friend was arguing the TNT would kill him. Both were wearing buttons that read: GRUMPEL'S: SERVICE WITH A CHEMICAL SMILE.

"You're both wrong!" Alfonse yelled. "Lewis will save him!"

"That's telling 'em, kid," Stephens growled as the trio passed the metal door and descended a spiral flight of stairs. They wound up in a corridor with walls of naked concrete, harsh, fluorescent lighting overhead, and a temperature so low they could see their breath. Far ahead, at the corridor's end, the bank manager was standing before a wall of gleaming metal. The XPJ.

"Fire Marshal Stephens!" the manager cried, brushing an imaginary speck from his jacket. "I hate to remind you, but we're running out of time. We have five minutes left."

"Five minutes and nineteen seconds," Stephens corrected. He nodded at Lewis. "All right, son, you've got your equipment. Now hop to it!"

"What ... what do you mean?" the manager sputtered. "Don't tell me you're relying on this ... this boy to do your job. Are you out of your mind?"

Ignoring the man's chatter, Lewis crouched beside the vault. It was an intimidating sight to say the least. Seven feet tall, three feet thick, and constructed from the latest space-age metal — for sure, the vault was impossible to open. He remembered when his mother displayed the blueprints and caused his dad to whistle in amazement.

Lewis shook himself free of these thoughts. Taking out his leather pouch, he selected the "bow and arrow" pick, a length of steel with a diamond-wedge tip. Using it to probe the base of the vault's handle — it looked a bit like a telephone receiver — he found a hairline crack in its surface and inserted the pick into this fissure. He rotated the tool clockwise until, *whoops*, the facing on the handle's base popped open. A hole appeared, no larger than a nickel.

"Whoa!" Alfonse and Stephens cried together.

Taking out his "dumbbell" pick, a shaft that ended in a metal ball, Lewis directed it into the hole until the ball came up against a hidden spring. There was a click as a metal "plug" gave way and revealed, below the handle, a two-inch "drain."

"Three more minutes," the manager announced. "I hope you're satisfied, Marshal Stephens. A man will die because of you. As for this boy —" he glared at Lewis "— I'll see to it personally that the police are informed."

"Ignore him, kid," Stephens whispered. "You're doing great."

Lewis tapped Alfonse. His friend deftly slipped him the wire, the paper clip, and a wad of chewed-up gum. Securing the gum to the wire's end, Lewis bent the clip into a thirty-degree angle, pressed it into the heart of the gum, and produced a makeshift fishing rod. That done, he pressed his ear against the door and steered the wire into the drain.

The manager groaned. "What will Mr. Grumpel say? Or our clients for that matter?"

"Please!" Lewis pleaded. "I need absolute quiet!"

"We can blow the vault still," the manager continued. "It's not too late!"

"Marshal Stephens," Lewis murmured, "I have to hear the timing mechanism. Can you keep this man quiet for the next sixty seconds?"

Stephens grinned. "My pleasure, kid."

"Now look here —" the manager began, only to fall silent as Stephens pressed a hand against his mouth.

"Here's the tricky bit," Lewis muttered, shoving the "fishing rod" into the depths of the vault. As he wiggled the wire, he "tickled" the X in the XPJ logo with his "scalpel" pick. Without warning a high-pitched whine broke out. "That noise means the chronometer has been neutralized. Now if I can wedge the paper clip into the stabilizing sensor ..."

"I don't mean to hurry you, kid," Stephens grunted, "but this had better work soon."

"There!" Lewis cried as a grinding sound erupted. "Try pulling the handle."

Throwing Lewis a look of disbelief, Stephens released the manager and gave the handle a yank. When the metal yielded easily, he snorted in amazement.

"Hurray!" Alfonse shouted.

"Huh?" the marshal said.

"Free at last!" a man gasped from inside, then collapsed onto the floor. His hands were swollen from banging them against the door and his face was purple. A canvas bag, bursting with hundred-dollar bills, lay at his feet.

There were suddenly lots of people in the hallway. Two medics were feeding oxygen to the thief, three cops were placing him under arrest, the clerks from upstairs were handling the money, and spectators were taking the confusion in. The fire marshal wanted to congratulate Lewis, but the manager told him that if he didn't deal with the crowd he would be held responsible if a single dollar went missing.

Lewis put his picks away. As soon as the pouch was in his pocket, he and Alfonse made their way to the staircase, dodging in and out of everyone. They were just about to mount the stairs when a light engulfed them and a microphone appeared.

"What's your name?" the reporter asked, even as her crew filmed the proceedings.

"Uh, Lewis Castorman."

"How old are you, Lewis?"

"I just turned twelve."

"Is it true you opened a vault with a paper clip, wire, and a stick of chewing gum?"

"Yes, but it was no big deal."

"Where did you learn to pick locks like that?"

"My dad's a locksmith. He taught me lots of stuff."

"I see. Tell me, Lewis —"

Sensing his friend's nervousness, Alfonse yelled, "Excuse us, please, we're late for school!" That said, he shoved the reporter aside and practically hauled Lewis up the stairs, through the lobby, and into the fresh spring air.

No one noticed as they hurried from the scene. They rushed down Grumpel Way and turned right on Grumpel Boulevard as Alfonse kept repeating how great Lewis had been, how the bank would reward him, and how they could use the money to buy stacks and stacks of comics.

Lewis smiled weakly. Although pleased his friend was impressed with his talents, he kept picturing the thief inside the vault. The man's face had been a ghastly shade of blue, his hands had been swollen, broken maybe, and his eyes had betrayed such intense desperation. Maybe Lewis's father was in a similar bind, only there wasn't anyone to rescue him.

His mind was made up. Lewis would phone the police as soon as he got home.

CHAPTER 3

When they entered their school, sweating hard and out of breath, Lewis and Alfonse debated their best course of action. They could go to the office where, because they were late, a secretary would mark them down for "Grumpel Service." This service was performed at nine each morning and required students who had done something wrong to compose a speech in praise of Ernst K. Grumpel, the founder and president-for-life of the school. Because the idea of singing his praises sickened them both, they decided to wait until the school broke for recess, at which point they would mix with the rest of the students and pretend they had been attending classes all along. In the meantime they would hide and read *Radiation Stories*, Alfonse's latest comic book purchase.

As they moved off to the boiler room, who should spy them but Frederick Winbag?

Mr. Winbag was their principal. Lewis had often wondered why this man was working in a school of all places. The qualities you would expect of a great principal — patience, kindness, a willingness to listen — were exactly the virtues Mr. Winbag lacked. Lewis suspected he had been a sergeant in his youth, whose job had been to break the spirits of the people beneath him.

It didn't help that Mr. Winbag seemed … unstable. His legs were like matchsticks, but his torso was massive, with an inflated gut that sagged to his knees. His head was as round as a soccer ball, with two popping eyes, a wet red mouth, and a nose that looked like a hunk of cheese. He also wore heavy glasses, which magnified his bulging eyeballs.

"What's this?" he now demanded, his claw-like hands descending on their shoulders.

"Good morning, Mr. Winbag," the boys said together.

"Are you arriving just now?" he asked, cracking their bones.

"There was an accident at the bank, sir," Alfonse gasped.

"You dare," Mr. Winbag said in a voice that sounded like a knife being sharpened, "you *dare* enter Mr. Grumpel's school forty-three and a half minutes late?"

Alfonse winced. "A man was trapped inside a vault. He would have —"

"Do you know how much you owe Mr. Grumpel?" Winbag rumbled, "He's built a school and hired teachers so spoiled brats like you can work for him one day."

"You don't understand!" Alfonse insisted. "Lewis saved someone's life this morning!"

"How dare you contradict!" Winbag shrieked. "Come with me!"

Moving quickly despite his clumsy frame, he led the boys down an immaculate hallway and past a seven-foot statue of Ernst K. Grumpel and walls that were covered with framed pictures and clippings. Each picture showed Grumpel shaking hands with politicians and receiving a prize for some chemical discovery. The clippings reported stories about his past, from his days as a pharmacist in Mason Springs to his present job as CEO and president of Grumpel Chemicals.

One clipping had always struck Lewis's notice. It recounted how, some five years earlier, a meteorite had landed on the chemist's farm — an ordinary stone according to Grumpel's reports. Two weeks later he had produced his first invention (a tonic that restored men's hair), and from that point on his fortunes had been sealed. Lewis had always found it strange that the chemist had met with success so soon after this stone's appearance.

"Don't move!" Winbag ordered, standing them in front of the maintenance room. Keeping one popping eye on them, he took a jar of polish and some rags from the closet. "Hold this!" he cried, filling their hands with this stuff. Grabbing them again, he swept them past a door that had been locked for as long as Lewis could remember. It led to a swimming pool that had been drained years earlier. The room was strictly off limits to students.

Lewis frowned as he studied the door. Its chain was hanging at a different angle — a locksmith is trained to notice such details — and that meant someone had recently entered the room. Was Grumpel intending to reopen the pool?

Before Lewis could say a word to Alfonse, Winbag hauled them out the school's front entrance and deposited them below an enormous sign. ERNST K. GRUMPEL SCHOOL, the gleaming two-foot letters read.

"Take these rags," the principal said, "and polish each letter until I can see my reflection. Maybe then you'll learn to appreciate Mr. Grumpel's generosity."

These orders given, Winbag returned inside. The boys rubbed their shoulders and exchanged bitter looks. The job was enormous. Some of the letters were within easy reach — the ones that spelled out SCHOOL, for example — but ERNST K. GRUMPEL was six feet off the ground and would be hard to clean without a ladder.

"I'll stand on your shoulders," Alfonse suggested. "We'll switch later on."

"We have no choice," Lewis agreed, wondering if his friend would be able to lift him.

"And all because you saved a life," Alfonse muttered. "Too bad I'm not The Bombardier. With a single proton exhalation, Winbag would catch fire and start begging for mercy."

"Daydreaming won't help. Let's get started."

For the next two hours they worked on the sign. The letters hadn't been cleaned in ages, and it took a lot of elbow grease to bring them to a shine. Lewis's shoulders ached from supporting Alfonse. At one stage, while polishing the *G* in *Grumpel*, his friend scrubbed so hard that he pitched Lewis off balance. Both went tumbling into a nearby bush.

"What's going on?" Winbag demanded, exiting the school just then. "I can't trust you with a simple job!" He stopped in mid-sentence and bowed to the ground. Surprised, the boys spun on their heels.

They should have known. Striding up the path was Elizabeth Grumpel, the chemist's daughter. As usual she wasn't alone: four masked bodyguards had her surrounded, and beside the curb was a sea-green limousine, sleek, sinewy, and like a shark.

"Good morning," Winbag said in his oiliest tone.

"Hi," she answered dismissively, studying her reflection in the letter *H* of *School*. As always, she looked perfect. Tall and athletic, she was dressed in an outfit her father had designed. It was waterproof, wrinkle-proof, dirt-proof, windproof, crease-proof, fireproof, and virtually indestructible. The outfit also changed colour every couple of minutes, as did the chemicals on her nails and hair. Just then she projected a fire-engine red.

"I trust the drive in from your estate was relaxing?" Winbag asked.

"It was awful," she replied, stroking a silver charm around her neck. "There was a disturbance in the bank, and I was delayed. I stopped off for cocoa to settle my nerves." She caught sight of Lewis just then. From boredom her expression changed to one of loathing.

Elizabeth Grumpel was a genuine bully. Every day a student would develop a rash, or see things in reverse, or grow hair on his palms, courtesy of potions from her father's lab. Because Lewis had once put out a fire that had broken out on someone's shoes — Elizabeth had coated them with a cream called Pyromania — she hated him intensely and was bent on getting even.

"I'm sorry you were delayed," Winbag said, "and you were wise to get yourself a cup of cocoa. When you see your father next, please send him my regards."

But Elizabeth had already turned her back on

Winbag and was entering the school with her guards in tow. She was eating a candy — a protein cube from Grumpel's Food Division — and had "accidentally" let the wrapper fall.

"Pick that up!" Winbag yelled at Lewis. "And polish *Grumpel* before you leave for class — the *m* and *p* aren't shiny enough! And if you're late again by so much as a second, I'll make you clean every brick on this building!"

A few minutes later the boys entered their classroom, having to pass the bodyguards who were watching the door. Their teacher, Ms. Widget, eyed them disapprovingly as they quietly took a seat at their desks. Students were reading from their compositions. The topic was "What My Parents Do for a Living."

Patricia Lagoon was informing everyone how her father was a dentist, only Grumpel Medics owned his practice and helped itself to half his money. "A fair arrangement," Ms. Widget exclaimed. Patricia's mother was a gardener, and because Grumpel Greens was the only nursery in town, she happened to work for the chemist, as well.

Lewis wasn't listening. Instead he was thinking of the boy at the bank and how he had come so close to losing his father, the bank thief. The thought almost made him sick to his stomach.

Bertie Spatula was next. His father was a tailor and dressed the males of Mason Springs. Because he leased his store from Grumpel, he had to pay the chemist a monthly tax. Grumpel also owned his mother's bookshop and decided the type of books she could sell.

Lewis frowned. He was remembering again the bank thief's purple complexion and thinking his father needed rescuing, too. Where was he? Where? Why hadn't he called?

Bill Silver, Jane Trumpet, Sarah Pfisker, John Pumpkin — all of them discussed their parents in turn, describing their positions as mechanics, plumbers, teachers, doctors ... All these people worked for Grumpel, and that was why they were paid so poorly and were forced to clock in the most gruelling hours.

Lewis smiled grimly to himself. He had always thought these families were uninteresting, that their jobs were boring and run-of-the-mill, while his parents' work was challenging and different. But at least these families were intact, whereas his father was absent and —

He started. Elizabeth Grumpel was at the front of the class, stroking her charm and regarding the crowd with a sneer.

"As you know," she began, her hair and dress a sunny yellow, "your families depend on my father for a living. If he wanted to, he could sack your parents, and it would serve them right, considering their lazy ..."

Lewis could sense Alfonse's mounting anger. It was bad enough he seldom got to see his parents, and all because Grumpel charged a vast sum of rent, but to hear his daughter run them into the ground, well, that was unendurable.

"But never mind that," she rambled on. "The main point is my father's products can be found in every house across the globe. Name a recent chemical substance, from cleaners to medicine to special kinds of glue, and you'll find the name 'Grumpel' printed on its label, because my father's a genius who —"

"A genius who's running out of steam!" Alfonse yelled, unable to contain himself.

"Be quiet, Alfonse!" Ms. Widget growled.

"But it's true," he insisted. "I read it in the paper. He's shutting all his factories down."

"How dare you!" Ms. Widget shrieked, slapping his desk with a large wooden ruler. "You'll be performing Grumpel Service for the next two years! Please carry on," she crooned to Elizabeth. "And I apologize for this unseemly outburst."

Elizabeth shrugged. "That's okay. People are jealous of my father's achievements. And speaking of achievements, I have something to show you. It's called a Petriglobe. Strike someone with it and you'll turn him into stone."

"Big deal," Alfonse jeered.

"Hold your tongue!" Ms. Widget screamed, smashing down her ruler again.

"Don't worry," Elizabeth chortled. "I'll handle this runt."

As Alfonse glared at her, she pulled a small orange sphere from her pocket and held it up for everyone to see. It looked a lot like a ball of gum. As the class eyed her quizzically, she tossed the sphere at Alfonse, who was on his feet and glaring at her still. The ball exploded, and a mist filled the room. The students recoiled and screamed in fear, only to start laughing when the fumes finally cleared.

Lewis flinched. His friend was frozen in a comic posture, hands raised in front of his face, eyes bulging wide in terror. To make things worse, his face, tie, jacket, hands, and hair were orange.

Elizabeth chuckled, tapping a nail against his cheek. "You see, he's trapped in a micro-fine layer of metal, thick enough to hold him, yet thin enough to let him breathe."

Ms. Widget laughed. "Very clever, but can you change him back to normal, dear?"

"No problem. Watch." Elizabeth revealed a vial with yellow liquid inside. Unscrewing its cap, she sprayed Alfonse with a couple of drops. Instantly, the metal coating melted, producing the scent of oranges, carrots, and squash. Alfonse himself shivered slightly, and his nose and fingers were still a vivid orange.

"Thank you, Elizabeth!" Ms. Widget cried as the students applauded. "Who's next? Lewis, we haven't heard from you."

Lewis winced and took his composition out. Walking to the front of the class, he cleared his throat and started to read. "My father is a locksmith. There isn't a lock in existence he can't open. While he often does what other locksmiths do, he usually performs specialty jobs and opens vaults, machines, and complicated engines whenever their locking systems fail."

"Wow!" Elizabeth drawled, pretending to yawn.

"Three years ago," Lewis read on, "he rescued the president of the United States when the locks in the Oval Office jammed. And last year, when the Canadian prime minister's jet had problems, he flew to it in a second plane and released the lock on its wheels in mid-air."

"How unusual," Ms. Widget said. "Now tell us about your mother."

Everyone stiffened, Elizabeth included. Ms. Widget was new to the school — she had been hired three months earlier to replace a teacher who had asked for a raise. As a result, she didn't know Lewis's history well.

"M-my m-mother?" Lewis stammered.

"Go on," Ms. Widget said, glancing at her watch.

"My mother ..." Lewis faltered, not knowing what to say.

The night he had been told his mother was gone, he had felt for the first time a weight pull him down, and had suspected there was nothing solid to rely on, that beneath his routines, his family and friends, there was nothing but a layer of ... blackness and fog. To stop himself from brooding on such thoughts, he had refused to discuss his mother with people — his father, their tenants, and Alfonse included. The kids at school, even Elizabeth Grumpel, had been happy to leave the subject alone, and his mother hadn't come up in their talk ... until now.

"Well?" Ms. Widget pressed.

"My mother ..." he repeated, unable to dispel his shock.

"We haven't got all day!" the teacher squawked.

He focused hard. A memory struck home. A few years back his mother had shown him a model of the XPJ. He remembered how she had laughed when he figured out how to open its drain.

"For the last time, hurry up!"

"My mother was a locksmith, too," Lewis finally said.

"She designed all sorts of different locks, ones impossible to open except for someone like my dad. My parents were always betting in a friendly way that she couldn't build a lock my father couldn't pick."

Ms. Widget sniffed. "How strange. But you say she *was* a locksmith?"

"She disappeared," Lewis mumbled.

"I beg your pardon?"

"I said she disappeared! A year ago she was working on a job — it was something she wasn't allowed to discuss. There was an accident and … and she never came home."

"I see," Ms. Widget observed, again consulting her watch.

"She was from Canada," Elizabeth snorted. "Everyone knows Canadians are dumb."

Lewis reacted so quickly that his motions were a blur. He gave Elizabeth's desk a kick, causing it to twist and pin her feet together. At the same time he lifted two wooden chairs and passed their legs across her torso, at an angle that wedged them fast against each other. As hard as she struggled, she was hopelessly trapped. By now her clothes and hair were jet-black.

"Get these off, or you'll be sorry!" she screamed.

"I learned this from my dumb Canadian mother," Lewis jeered.

"Guards!" Elizabeth yelled, straining at the chairs. "Get in here and rescue me!"

"Hurray!" Alfonse cheered. "That should teach her a lesson!"

"Don't panic, dear," Ms. Widget volunteered, even

as the guards bowled into the room. Brushing the frantic teacher aside, they grabbed the chairs and tried to pull them apart. But they wouldn't budge.

"What's the matter?" Elizabeth shrieked. "I thought you guys were strong!"

"Let's work together," Ms. Widget said, motioning the students to help the guards. The children, except Alfonse, pulled as hard as they could, but their efforts only made the situation worse. The more they strained the more the chairs squeezed together, and the bluer Elizabeth grew in the face.

Ms. Widget wheeled on Lewis. "Get these off, or I'll have you arrested!"

"You heard her, punk," a bodyguard grunted, his breath causing his mask to puff out.

"I'm not lifting a finger," Lewis said, "until *she* apologizes for insulting my mother."

"It's not my fault your mother's Canadian!" Elizabeth cried.

"Have it your way," Lewis said, stepping away from the scene.

Alfonse clapped. "That's telling her, Lewis!"

"All right, I'm sorry," Elizabeth snarled. "Now get rid of these chairs!"

Without a word Lewis approached her desk. The students and guards stepped aside and watched as he gripped the chairs and squeezed them together. They separated instantly. He then straightened the desk and freed Elizabeth's legs.

"Are you okay, dear?" Ms. Widget asked worriedly.

"No! I'm *not* okay!" she yelled. "These chairs have

cut my circulation off!"

"Let me take you to the nurse," Ms. Widget crooned, leading Elizabeth to the classroom door. Before exiting the room she wheeled on Lewis and roared, "As for *you*, Lewis Castorman, that stunt will cost you dearly! For the next four weeks you'll remain after school. Maybe that will teach you to respect your betters."

"This isn't fair!" Alfonse protested. "She insulted his mother!"

"Is that so?" Ms. Widget growled. "Then you can share his detention with him!"

Lewis and Elizabeth exchanged acid glances. Even as she sneered at him — her clothes and hair were a bright lime-green — he was thinking his trick was worth ten years of detention.

CHAPTER 4

It was 6:45 p.m. Lewis was on the porch and trading stares with an oak. The air was warm, a chorus of crickets was chirping, and the fumes from a barbecue were making him faint with hunger. All in all, the atmosphere was tranquil, but he was feeling … lousy.

Never mind that Ms. Widget had kept him after school and had forced him to write five hundred lines on the board — "I apologize for my rude and ungrateful behaviour." And never mind that Mrs. Gibson had cooked a ghastly meal — meat loaf and potato peels — as a quick peek in the kitchen had revealed. It was really the silent phone that had him down in the dumps.

How was it possible? he kept asking himself How could lightning strike a household twice? First, his mother had vanished without trace, and now his father had fallen off the face of the planet? Was fate bent on wiping the Castormans out?

A curtain stirred. Mrs. Gibson. She had been looking very anxious all evening, while Mr. Todrey had gone walking to settle his nerves.

Lewis sighed. He would wait until 7:00 p.m., at which point he would report his missing dad to the police. How would they respond? Would a car appear with a pair of detectives who would ask lots of questions and search his dad's belongings? Would the neighbours stand outside their doors, the parents clutching their kids, and shake their heads in consternation and mutter they had always known there was something weird about that house? And would a hard-faced woman knock at the door, drenched in Grumpel's Number Four Perfume, and conduct him to an orphanage now that both his parents were missing?

His chest felt hollow. His tongue was all shrivelled. Would he be forced to leave? Would he see Alfonse? And what would the two tenants do?

The phone rang. His heart exploded. Racing inside, he pounced on the receiver. "Hello?"

"Are you watching the news?" Alfonse cried. Adelaide was playing the piano in the background.

"I'm waiting for my dad to call," Lewis groaned. "He still —"

"Turn the TV on! Go to Channel 14!"

"I'm going to phone the police —"

"Hurry! You'll miss it otherwise!"

Hanging up, Lewis engaged the TV. He gasped when he saw his face filling the screen.

"Is it true," the reporter from the bank was asking, "that you opened a vault with a paper clip, wire, and a stick of chewing gum?"

"Yes," his TV twin replied, "but it was no big deal."

He had been so worried about his father that he had forgotten the bank. How odd he seemed in front of the camera, with the firemen and cops scurrying all over. His pride quickened. That was *him* on TV — Lewis Seymour

Castorman! How many locksmiths, let alone kids, could open an XPJ using such basic equipment? He was pretty smart, wasn't he?

"Where did you learn to pick locks like that?"

"My dad's a locksmith. He taught me lots of stuff."

At this mention of his father, Lewis instantly deflated. So he had opened an XPJ — big deal. His father was missing. Something dreadful was wrong. As the reporter jabbered on about Lewis's great achievement, he frowned and switched the TV off. It was time to call the police, no matter what, even if it meant sleeping in an orphanage that evening. His hand reached out to pick up the receiver when the phone started ringing a second time.

"Alfonse," Lewis said, "I can't speak now —"

"Is this Lewis Castorman?" a low, commanding voice inquired.

"Oh. Sorry. This is Lewis. Who's speaking please?"

"This is Ernst K. Grumpel, CEO of Grumpel Chemicals."

Lewis was thunderstruck. Ernst K. Grumpel? Why would he be calling? Elizabeth must have told him about his stunt with the chairs. It wasn't enough that his father was missing, but now he was in trouble with the chemist, as well!

"Are you there?" Grumpel rasped.

"Yes, sir. And about this afternoon, I'm afraid your daughter and I —"

"Yes, quite," the chemist rumbled. "An accident, I'm sure. Now see here, Lewis. I saw your story on TV, and to be frank, young man, I'm deeply impressed. Your work today was, simply put, outstanding."

"I see. Thank you, sir."

"In fact, I was telling your father —"

"My father? You saw my father?"

"Of course. He's been working here these past few days, and I was telling him —"

"Can I speak to him?"

"Unfortunately, he's tied up now. But why don't you visit me in New York City tomorrow? I have a proposition to make, and afterward you can talk to your father."

"Great!" Lewis cried, his fingers shaking with excitement.

"Excellent. A car will pick you up at 8:00 a.m. And don't worry about school — I'll arrange everything with Mr. Winbag. All right?"

"That's fantastic! I mean, thank you very much. And tell my dad —"

But the chemist had hung up already.

For a moment Lewis was at a loss — a minute earlier there had been no hope, whereas now ... He whooped and turned a cartwheel in the living room, scattering a pile of books in the process. Mrs. Gibson hurried in from the kitchen and asked if he had been in touch with his father. Turning another cartwheel and upsetting a plant, Lewis explained that his father was fine and that Mr. Grumpel had invited him to New York City. With one final cartwheel, which knocked a picture off its hook, he ran to the phone to tell Alfonse the good news.

Mrs. Gibson reached it first. With a cry of panic she ripped it from the wall. A moment later she was scrambling all over, closing windows, locking the front door, and drawing curtains that hadn't been dusted in ages. And as soon as she had bolted the door in the kitchen, she returned to the living room with a spatula in hand.

"I knew something was wrong," she said. "But this is worse than I imagined!"

"You don't understand," Lewis explained, not knowing what to make of her behaviour. "Mr. Grumpel said my father's —"

"He's laying a trap! Your life is in danger!"

Lewis laughed. "That's ridiculous! Why would Grumpel —"

"He's after something! Believe me, I know!"

"Let's discuss this over supper," Lewis suggested, even as he cringed at the smells in the kitchen. "As soon as we've eaten, you'll feel a lot calmer."

"I'll make you understand!" she announced in a tone that was different from her normal way of speaking. She raised her hands, and in one brusque motion snatched her bright orange hair away — so her curls *had* been a mop all along! As Lewis's mouth dropped open in shock, she pulled a rag from her apron pocket and gave her face a couple of scrubs, wiping off the talcum powder to disclose a greenish-brown and scaly skin beneath.

As hard as Lewis tried to speak, not a word would come out.

She wasn't done yet. Biting down on the finger of one glove, she removed its rubber to reveal a ... flipper. Her gloves off, she wrestled with the ring on her neck until it loosened with a sucking sound and her face collapsed and was no longer human. Long it was and saggy and brown, as if she were … an oversized frog!

Lewis ran for the door.

"Lewis! Wait!" the creature pleaded, plodding after him.

The thermal lock — why wouldn't it open?

"Lewis! Please! Let me explain!"

The giant creature was three feet away, with a long tongue dangling between its jaws. As it tried to grab Lewis, the thermal lock jumped open and he rolled past the door with half a second to spare. Scrambling across the porch, he jumped to his freedom.

Only to knock into a lurking figure.

"Mr. Todrey! Run!" he yelled, crashing into the tenant, who dropped an armload of books. "That isn't Mrs. Gibson, but —"

"Gibiwink!" Mr. Todrey growled, spying the creature. "What's going on?"

"Just run!" Lewis cried. "Wait! Did you call this creature Gibiwink?"

Mr. Todrey grabbed Lewis and hurled him inside. Dropping him onto the living-room couch, he seized "Gibiwink" by the apron strings. "What's going on?" he thundered.

"Grumpel called!" Gibiwink whimpered. "He's invited Lewis to New York City."

Mr. Todrey's mouth dropped open, and he let out a shriek. An instant later he was leaping around the house and checking that all the doors and windows were locked. In his panic he didn't duck when he drew near the kitchen, and there was a painful crash as his head struck the lintel. The impact shook his moustache free — the skin beneath was brown and scaly.

Mr. Todrey was an alien, too!

Despite his panic, Lewis struggled to his feet. "Mr. Todrey" was sprawled on the floor, and "Mrs. Gibson" was leaning over him. Neither of them noticed as Lewis stole to the door, fiddled with the lock, and —

"Lewis!" Gibiwink cried. "Todrus is bleeding! Could you get me a cloth?"

"Oh, my head," Todrus moaned. "Is it bad, Gibiwink?"

"Bad enough. Lewis, please, we could really use that cloth."

Lewis studied them from his place by the exit. Despite their strange, horrific appearance, he couldn't help but notice how gentle they seemed. In fact, far from being scary, both were shaking with terror. Against his better judgment, Lewis entered the kitchen. With a trembling hand he took a towel from the dish rack, soaked it in water, and approached the pair.

"Here," he said quietly, shuddering as he took them in — wartish, slimy, and dumpy they were, with close-set eyes, enormous mouths ...

"Thanks," Gibiwink murmured, pressing the cloth against Todrus's skull.

"That's better," Todrus sighed. "Now if the two of you could help me to the couch ..."

Feeling he had no choice in the matter, Lewis helped Todrus to his feet. It wasn't easy. The tenant weighed four hundred pounds and was reeling still from the effects of his collision. When they dropped him onto the couch, all three of them were panting.

"I'm sorry if we startled you," the former Mr. Todrey said, the towel pressed against his cut. "Let us introduce ourselves. I'm Todrus, and he's Gibiwink. He's a male, like me."

"A pleasure, Lewis," Gibiwink said.

"L-likewise," Lewis quavered.

Todrus sighed. "And you're owed an explanation. You want to know what giant, talking frogs are doing in your living room, right?"

"Uh, well, yes."

"You've heard of Yellow Swamp in Alberta, Canada?"

Lewis nodded. Who hadn't heard of Yellow Swamp? It had suffered a chemical spill the year before and had been damaged beyond all hope of recognition. According to newspaper reports, the region was so strange and unstable that no one dared go anywhere near it. At the same time, a year before the spill had taken place, the Castormans had actually camped in Yellow Swamp. His mother had known about it because she had grown up in Alberta.

"We lived there," Todrus said, "before the 'accident' happened. We were ordinary wood frogs then, tiny creatures that didn't speak any English —"

"Until *they* came," Gibiwink broke in.

Todrus nodded. "That's right. One morning, without warning, three helicopters landed near Yellow Swamp. A group of big, masked men emerged — one look at them and we knew they meant serious business. An unmasked woman appeared, as well, and following her commands, these figures set to work opening boxes and taking things over."

"The noise!" Gibiwink complained. "Before their arrival our swamp was peaceful, but they started digging trenches and laying pipes in the soil."

"Days they toiled," Todrus agreed. "Drilling, digging, cutting, welding, as if the swamp were theirs to treat as they pleased. At one point one of them just about killed us. He was drilling near our log and would have cut us to pieces. Luckily, that woman was watching him closely and saved us in the nick of time."

"She fed us after that," Gibiwink added. "Each morning she'd leave us crumbs from her breakfast."

"And she was always singing," Todrus mused, "from the moment she got up until late in the evening."

A car passed and cast its lights in the room. Quick as thought, the frogs hit the floor. They hissed at him to hide, as well, but Lewis approached the window and glanced outside. "It's the Pangettis. They're coming home from work."

"We're jumpy since the accident," Gibiwink explained.

"The accident," Todrus groaned, regaining his place on the couch, "happened three weeks after their arrival. The woman had put on a diving suit and was inspecting the pipes that had been laid in the swamp. The masked men took advantage of her absence. While she was swimming beneath the surface, they climbed into the helicopters and abandoned her — the thugs!"

"One helicopter climbed above the swamp," Gibiwink continued, his voice low and full of sadness. "A door slid open, and two figures appeared. Without wasting time they shoved a stone overboard — huge it was, about the size I am now, only brilliantly coloured and shaped like an egg. It plunged into the middle of the swamp. The other two helicopters sprayed a bright yellow dust, which hung above the swamp like an old, shabby curtain. *That's* when everything started to change."

"Change?" Lewis asked.

Todrus shuddered. "Yes. Just minutes after the dust broke out, the swamp turned orange and started to boil. At the same time a fog rose up — a red-brown gas you could have cut with a knife — and covered the sky as if it were evening. It was the strangest sight I've ever seen."

"More important," Gibiwink added, "that's when *we* transformed. I mean, one moment we were wood frogs, small and stupid-looking; then a bolt of lightning struck and ... everything made sense. I mean, both of us could think and even speak the odd word."

"And we were growing," Todrus said. "We'd tripled in size."

The frogs swallowed hard.

Lewis cleared his throat. "What about the woman?"

Todrus gulped. "When she surfaced from the swamp and spied the bright orange water and the bank of fog, she was frightened and kept her diving suit on. She also screamed when she saw that the helicopters were gone. At the same time she was standing in this reddish foam — a lot like a bubble bath only it seemed to be breathing. As she tried to make her way onto the shore, these suds grabbed hold of her and ... and wouldn't let go."

"We tried to save her," Gibiwink moaned. "Even though the swamp was boiling, we rowed our log toward her ..."

"But we scared her," Todrus said. "We were five feet tall and growing still, and how could she know we wanted to help? We understood English, from having heard it spoken, but could barely speak a word just then. Eventually, with signals, we explained ourselves. When she finally grabbed our flippers, it was too late. As hard as we pulled, the suds wouldn't free her. They were past her shoulders and —"

The frogs fell silent. They were clearly upset. To allow them time to recover their spirits, Lewis glanced outside and exchanged stares with the moon. He was thinking the world was ... precarious. His mother was gone. His dad was in danger. Yellow Swamp had been turned into a wasteland. And now there were talking giant frogs to deal with. What was happening? Why was everything so upside down?

"Where were we?" Todrus asked.

"The woman," Lewis prodded him, "she was trapped in the suds?"

"She realized it was useless," Todrus continued, "and urged us to leave before the swamp sucked us under. At the same time she asked for one last favour. She motioned to a locket around her neck and begged us to take it to her son in Mason Springs — in the United States of America, she explained. We were to tell him and her husband how she had died in Yellow Swamp, and that ... that she loved them both with all her heart. No sooner had we grabbed the locket than the earth shook violently and the suds —"

"No!" Gibiwink declared. "Before she vanished she managed to yell, 'This is Ernst K. Grumpel's doing! Be careful, or he'll kill you, too!' And then she was gone."

"After that," Todrus whispered, "we had various adventures, which I won't go into. The point is, we left Canada and made our way down here, where we tracked that woman's family down, disguised as Mr. Todrey and Mrs. Gibson."

"Y-you mean …" Lewis stammered, putting two and two together.

"Yes," Todrus said, "that woman was none other than your mother."

Lewis's head reeled. So his mother hadn't simply disappeared. According to these frogs, she had been brutally murdered! All her love and kindness and wisdom — someone had deliberately smashed these to pieces!

No, not someone. Ernst K. Grumpel.

Todrus held up a golden locket. "Look!"

Seizing it, Lewis pried its cover open. Inside was a family portrait. Lewis instantly recalled the occasion: his family had been vacationing in Montreal and had stopped off in a photo booth where this picture had been taken. Blind to the future, the three of them were smiling.

"When your father heard our story," Todrus continued, "he invited us to live with you. He knew Grumpel might otherwise hunt us down to keep his antics in Yellow Swamp a secret."

Lewis nodded. Studying the picture, he felt hot and cold at once. He was the son of someone who had been ruthlessly killed, and this piece of information changed his place in the world.

"Why didn't you go to the police?" he asked in a voice that sounded like paper being crinkled.

"Who would have believed us?" Todrus asked. "It was our word against Grumpel's, the world's most powerful businessman."

"We'd have wound up in jail," Gibiwink added, "if Grumpel hadn't gotten to us first."

Lewis's head was spinning. He had so many questions. Why hadn't his father taken action against Grumpel? Why was he working for the man who had killed his wife? What was *he* supposed to do when Grumpel's car drove him to the city the next day?

"That's enough for now," Todrus said, understanding Lewis's confusion. "It's late and we should eat something. Let's discuss our plans over a nice hot supper."

"Good idea," Gibiwink said. "There's nothing like my meat loaf to set a person's thinking straight!"

CHAPTER 5

When Lewis awoke the following morning, he thought he had had an interesting dream. He smiled broadly as he remembered the details — a tale about frogs, chemicals, and Yellow Swamp — until he felt something hard poking his side. Reaching out, he found it smooth to the touch, oddly shaped, too, with webbing and —

He glanced down. The frogs were sleeping on the floor beside him. Gibiwink's arm was sprawled across the sheets, and his flipper was digging into Lewis. The events from the previous night returned in a flash.

He checked the clock — a quarter to seven. Retrieving his clothes, he dressed in a hurry, headed downstairs, and wrote a brief note: "Back in ten minutes." Opening the thermal lock, he ran outside.

A minute later he was on the Pangettis' lawn and tossing pebbles at Alfonse's window. Shortly after, wrestling with a shirt and tie, his friend joined him in the yard below.

"Grumpel phoned last night," Lewis told him. "He wants me to visit him in New York City this morning."

"Grumpel? New York City? You've got to be kidding!"

"He saw me on TV and wants to speak to me in person. He mentioned, too, that my dad's been working for him."

"That's great! So there's no reason to worry?"

"Wait. There's more."

Hardly believing the details himself, Lewis summarized the frogs' strange tale. When he ended with the news that his mother had been murdered, and that Grumpel himself had committed the crime, in addition to creating the Yellow Swamp disaster, Alfonse looked ... skeptical.

"In other words," Lewis concluded as they approached the front door of his house, "Grumpel's dangerous and probably means trouble. So what do you think? Should I stay or go?"

"I think," Alfonse said, "that you could write one heck of a comic."

"I'm being serious!"

"So am I. Your story has everything a good comic needs — a mad scientist, weird experiments, murder, intrigue —"

"Have it your way!" Lewis shrugged and walked into the house.

The frogs were up and busy in the kitchen. Because Gibiwink was stirring some oatmeal on the stove, his face was turned away from the boys. And Todrus was reading at the kitchen table, so his features were hidden behind the *Mason Springs Gazette*.

"Good morning," the frogs said without revealing themselves.

"Good morning," the boys answered. Alfonse took a seat at the table.

"Grumpel's closed another factory," Todrus told them. "That leaves him only with his New York operation. I'm telling you, there's something fishy going on."

"Mr. Todrey," Alfonse asked, "can I look at the comics?"

"In a minute. There's a story about Yellow Swamp in here, how the Canadians have blocked the area off — not even government officials are allowed inside."

"Lewis is working on a comic," Alfonse said, tossing Lewis a wink. "It's about frogs that are changed by a chemical cloud —"

"Here you go," Todrus said distractedly, handing him the paper and revealing his features.

At the same time Gibiwink brought the oatmeal to the table, visible in all his frog-like glory. "Some sugar?" he asked Alfonse, as if being addressed by a frog were an everyday occurrence.

Alfonse dropped the paper and drew back in his chair.

"We're confusing the boy," Todrus whispered. "Maybe we should —"

"There isn't time," Lewis interjected. "The car's due soon, and we have to reach a decision."

"I think it's risky," Todrus warned. "Grumpel means business."

"We should run away," Gibiwink agreed. "Before he manages to nab us."

"And my father?" Lewis argued. "What if he's in trouble?"

There was a pause, and the frogs glanced at each other. Lewis wanted to consult with Alfonse, but his friend looked as if he had been hit by a truck.

"Well, if you're going," Todrus insisted, "we're coming, too."

"We'll wear our disguises," Gibiwink added.

Lewis frowned. "I don't know. Grumpel might catch on. And from everything you've told me, he'll probably kill you."

"It makes no difference," Todrus insisted. "We owe your father everything, and a frog would rather die than live without honour. And by sticking together, the three of us —"

"The four of us," Alfonse croaked. "I'm coming, too."

"This isn't your problem," Lewis said. "There could be trouble ..."

"If you think you're going to hog this adventure for yourself, the most exciting thing to happen in Mason Springs in ages, I've got news for you, Mr. Lewis Castorman."

"All right," Lewis agreed, happy to have his friends onboard. "I'm glad —"

"After all," Alfonse interrupted, "what would The Bombardier say if he found out I'd bolted at the first sniff of danger?"

"Alfonse, I said you can come!" Lewis cried.

"Who do you think I am, the Human Glop or something?"

Alfonse would have rambled on had a horn not sounded — much to Lewis's relief.

They glanced outside. Parked before the driveway was a huge limousine, thirty feet long and powerful-looking, with sea-green chrome, black-tinted windows, and a golden figure mounted in front — a miniature statue of Ernst K. Grumpel. The chauffeur, dressed in red livery, his features masked, was leaning on the hood of the car. With a gold gloved hand he gave the horn a second blast.

"Remember," Todrus whispered, fitting on his moustache, "you can count on us one hundred percent."

"One hundred percent," Gibiwink echoed, his wig and metal brace in place.

Lewis and his three companions left the house and approached the car. The driver saluted smartly. "Which wun uv yuhs is Lewis Castorman?" he asked.

"I am," Lewis said, "but there's been a change. My friends are coming, too."

"Yeah? Says who?"

"Says me!" Lewis shot back.

"I'll havta check wid de boss," the chauffeur muttered. "He don't like surprises."

As the chauffeur ducked inside the car and grappled with a phone, Lewis poked Alfonse and motioned down the block — Alfonse's sister, Adelaide, was heading straight toward them.

"Oh, no!" Alfonse groaned. "That's all we need."

"What's going on?" she demanded. "Why's this limo on our street?"

"Who wants to know?" Alfonse snapped back.

"It's taking us to New York City," Lewis volunteered.

"Why?" Adelaide asked.

"It's complicated," Lewis said.

"What he means," Alfonse snarled, "is that it's none of your business!"

"Can I have a lift?" Adelaide asked. "I have a recital and would like to get to school early."

"Uh …" Lewis hesitated.

"No way!" Alfonse snapped. "We have better things to do."

"Okay, he agrees," the chauffeur spoke, back outside and opening a door. "We's can leave any time youse guys is ready."

"You're dropping me off," Adelaide said, despite her brother's protests.

The chauffeur smirked, motioning them in with a wave of his finger. "De more de merrier."

Although instinct told him something was wrong, Lewis ducked inside and sat by a window. Alfonse slid in beside him and gasped at the fittings: there was a small TV, a fridge at their feet, a neck massager on the back of each seat, and a collapsible tray for taking one's meals. As he fiddled with the TV set — it seemed to be broken — Lewis studied a pane of glass that kept them separate from the driver's cab. It was black and fitted with an intercom.

The frogs were motioning Adelaide forward. Despite their politeness, she was taken aback. She had never spied the pair close up, and their peculiar appearance made her uneasy.

"Quit stallin'!" the chauffeur yelled. "Yer holdin' up traffic!"

Adelaide finally climbed inside the car. Gibiwink and Todrus clambered in behind her, and as soon as they were seated, the driver started the engine. Instantly, the locks engaged.

"Those are Ambassador locks," Lewis whispered. "They're used in prison cells, not in limousines."

Alfonse sighed. "Relax. How often do you get to ride in such comfort?"

"And why this glass?" Lewis mused, tapping the divider between them and the driver. The car was gliding forward like a beast of prey.

"It's to give us privacy," Alfonse suggested.

"It's made of Ferroplex," Lewis said, "and is strong enough to resist the blows of a hammer. You don't find that strange?"

Alfonse yawned. "Look, this is America, Lewis. If Grumpel pulls a fast one, he'll get in trouble with the cops, so sit back and enjoy the ride."

Lewis wanted to remind his friend that Grumpel had murdered, *murdered*, his mother, and that his dad had probably been kidnapped or something. Before he could speak, Adelaide rapped the divider.

"Excuse me!" she shouted. "You missed the street for our school!"

"Hello!" Lewis said, speaking into the intercom. "We're dropping off my friend. Could you turn on Grumpel Crescent, please? It's two blocks down …"

The car was moving quickly. As it neared Grumpel Crescent, it kept muscling forward.

"Hey!" Todrus cried. "You've missed the turn again!"

"Can it, fatso!" the driver growled, his masked face appearing on the TV screen

"I beg your pardon?"

"Yuhs hoid me. I's ain't toinin' fuh no skool. No witnesses, dose are my orders."

"Stop the car!" Lewis yelled. "Stop this instant!"

But the driver only stepped on the gas. They were speeding toward the highway.

"What's going on?" Adelaide asked as Gibiwink flicked his tongue in and out.

"Pick the locks!" Todrus shouted. "If we can open a door, we can signal for help!"

Lewis pulled two picks from his wallet — a diamond point and a number seven. He stabbed the diamond point into the door's soft fabric, an inch below the window casing, and sawed a square of the padding away. The hole revealed the lock's internal workings — eight steel pins attached to a "spinner." Manoeuvring his second pick, he neutralized the pins one by one.

"Almost there!" he yelled. "Two more pins to go!"

"I's wudn't do dat," the driver said.

"Hurry, Lewis!" Todrus urged. "We're almost at the highway!"

"I'm on the last pin! There! Let's open the door!"

"I's warned yuhs!" the driver snarled.

As Lewis and Todrus threw their weight against the door and Gibiwink flicked his tongue in and out and Adelaide asked what was going on and Alfonse jabbered on about The Bombardier, a red gas wafted out from under the seats. Instantly, the group felt their muscles slacken.

The frogs collapsed to the floor of the car. Alfonse fell over with his feet in the air. Adelaide slithered against the back of the seat, repeating in her sleep, "What's going on? What's going on?" With a supreme act of will, Lewis kept his eyes open, but he couldn't move a finger … or open the door.

The driver laughed. "I's gots tuh hand it tuh yuhs, kid. Yuh soitenly know yer way around locks. But yuhs woint expectin' sleepin' gas, was yuhs? So say nighty night an' shut yer eyes an' I'll get yuhs tuh de boss safe 'n sound."

By now the limousine was whizzing along the highway, passing every car and truck on the road. Lewis felt as if he were watching a movie as he propped his head against the window and fields and farms zipped past in a blur. On and on the greenery sprawled, with the occasional farmer driving along on his tractor, or a herd of cows wandering in search of breakfast.

Most beautiful of all was the shadow on the horizon. Huge it was, miles long, and poised at its heart was a series of towers, whose sides were catching the odd sunbeam and reflecting its brilliance a hundred times over. New York City. Despite his dopiness, Lewis smiled weakly as he remembered how his family had visited the city, often in search of tools for their workshop. He had loved the crush and smell of the subway, the parade of characters in the various parks, the music jumping out from a hundred different corners, the feeling he was everywhere in the world at once, yet safe within the embrace of his parents … his parents … his parents …

Darkness hit him like a boxer's glove.

He awoke a while later. The limousine was in the heart of the city and stalled in a traffic jam of buses, cabs, and delivery trucks. The drivers were waving their hands impatiently, blaring their horns, and cursing everyone around them. Although the sky was glorious with not a cloud on the horizon, they were on an avenue that was immersed in shadow: a wall of buildings, each fifty storeys tall, was preventing the light from reaching the street. Shoulder to shoulder the skyscrapers stood, some stone, some metal, some broken-down, some sparkling new, like giants gathering to have their pictures taken.

Again Lewis tried to jimmy the lock. The limousine was entering the business district, and the sidewalks were packed with lines of New Yorkers who would stop the car and arrest the driver if Lewis could only attract their attention ...

"Watch dat, sonny," the driver growled, "or I'll gives yuhs anudder dose uv de gas. Besides, wer almost dere."

Taking advantage of a break in the traffic, the driver turned into a tiny lane — barely missing a truck — and barrelled past a row of buildings with fire escapes clinging to their walls like ivy. The car veered right, then left, then left again, down alleys that were ridiculously narrow, with bits of paper careering in its wake. As Lewis tried to get his bearings, the car stopped outside a heavy metal doorway. Above the plating, on a length of pitted limestone, a sign read: GRUMPEL CHEMICALS: DELIVERY ENTRANCE.

"This is it?" Lewis asked. He had been expecting something fancy, a stainless-steel tower with a gold-trimmed lobby perhaps, and not the plain, low structure that confronted them now. Sitting up, he shook the Pangettis awake. The frogs, for their part, were beginning to stir.

The metal door swung open. The limousine inched into a cramped garage, its dimensions barely large enough to contain the car. As soon as the car came to a standstill, the door closed behind them, leaving them in darkness. A hum started up — the garage was descending.

"Wake up, everyone!" Lewis cried. "We're almost there!"

"Where's there?" Alfonse groaned.

"I don't know. Somewhere underground in New York."

"What's going on?" Adelaide muttered, repeating her last train of thought.

The elevator stopped. There was a sharp, pneumatic hiss, and a door opened briskly, causing them to squint when light flooded the garage. The car rolled forward, then came to a stop. With an unnaturally loud click the locks disengaged. Lewis and Todrus opened a door and, hesitating briefly, stepped outside. The others followed closely behind.

Their mouths dropped open. Assembled in front of them, in ranks and columns, were thousands of workers dressed in spotless white outfits. This might not have been so unusual except that each was … an overgrown reptile.

Seven feet tall, muscular-looking, with diamond-shaped heads, light brown scales, and eyes that gleamed with a cold intelligence, they were an intimidating sight to say the least.

"I'm sleeping still," Adelaide groaned. "And dreaming about lizards."

"They aren't lizards," Todrus corrected her. "They're tiger salamanders. You often see them in the Yellow Swamp region, only they never grow so big."

"The chemical spill must have changed them," Gibiwink said. "But why are they here?"

"In *Bombardier 7*," Alfonse whispered, "Doc Camphor creates an army of spiders —"

"Shut up about your comics!" Adelaide snapped.

"No, he's right," Lewis murmured. "Grumpel has built himself a powerful army using the same chemicals that —

"Shhh," Todrus said to stop him from giving the frogs' secret away.

"Sorry," Lewis apologized, "but why do you think each of them is wearing a ring?" He was referring to a metal band clamped around each reptile's neck.

Then Alfonse called out, "Never mind the salamanders! Look above!"

Gazing upward, everyone gasped. They were standing in an enormous plaza. Four gleaming towers rose from its sides, each fifty storeys tall and containing hundreds of windows. Bridges connected each tower to its neighbour, level after level of them, and when the entire structure was viewed from below, it resembled an intricate spiderweb, only one the size of a miniature city.

Alfonse gulped. "This place is huge! It must have taken twenty years to build!"

"More like thirty," Gibiwink said. "Just digging underground would have taken forever."

"But Grumpel's been in business only five years," Todrus mused. "How?"

"There's your answer," Lewis said, pointing to five salamanders toiling nearby.

They were standing near a patch of earth, with what looked like an aerosol can between them. Spraying the earth with a bluish gas, they caused it to bubble and rapidly expand, and as it did, they sculpted it into a wall and cut out holes for the doors and windows.

They repeated this operation three more times, and very quickly produced a solid, handsome structure — a garage for the limousine to park in! With a chemical like this to speed things along, no wonder Grumpel had been able to build so swiftly.

Lewis was going to inspect the garage, but a band of salamander guards closed in. Each was armed with a strange-looking gun whose breech was loaded with coloured marbles.

"Petriglobes," Alfonse whispered.

The chauffeur laughed. "Dese guys will take good care of yuhs." He was a salamander, too. "I'd say good luck, but no luck's gonna save yuhs."

The guards shoved the group toward a nearby elevator. Moments later they were shooting skyward.

"Ooh!" Gibiwink squealed. "It's just like flying!"

"Why did Grumpel build this complex underground?" Lewis asked, staring at the plaza with its gleaming towers.

"He's hiding something," Alfonse said. "That's certainly true of Acid Master who has an underground fortress to keep his secrets safe —"

"Never mind that!" Adelaide broke in. "Why have we been kidnapped? What does Grumpel want from *us*?"

The elevator stopped near the top of the tower — just a couple of floors beneath the ground's surface. The door whooshed open, and the guards led them out. A hallway received them — it contained a series of doors. The walls were white and antiseptic, and the light overhead was hard on the eyes. At a signal from the salamanders the captives shuffled forward.

They walked for several minutes. No one spoke. There were signs on each door, and Lewis read them as he and his friends passed. NUCLEIC REACTIONS, one door read, then DEHYDRATION, COMBUSTION, CLONING, ORGANIC, PROTEIN, and METALLIZATION. At one point Lewis heard an assortment of sounds, pops in one case, as if bubbles were bursting, then the roar of blazing fires, followed by a faint explosion and … a bloodcurdling scream!

They also went by several groups of workers. All of them were idling about as if they hadn't any work to keep them busy. They, too, were wearing rings around their necks. An idea struck Lewis. "Those metal bands," he whispered, "I think Grumpel's using them to control these creatures."

"That's possible," Todrus agreed. "He could guide their thoughts with radio signals, and those metal bands would make the perfect receiver. Salamanders, too, are known to be unstable."

He would have said more, but they were brought to a stop.

They were standing before a massive door that looked like a gate on a medieval castle. The guards arranged the friends in a line, then the leader spoke into a box on the wall. A moment later the door opened slowly.

"Mr. Grumpel will now see you," the leader announced.

Nodding curtly, Lewis faced the door, inhaled deeply, and stepped inside. Something told him he would be lucky to escape this place alive.

CHAPTER 6

The office was the size of a baseball field. Not only were its walls a great distance from one another, but its ceiling was so outlandishly high that for a moment Lewis thought the sky was above him. The forbidding silence told him otherwise. Even on a quiet day there were always sounds outside: the hum of traffic, an excitable dog, the wind rustling the leaves on a tree. In this space there was no noise whatsoever. The silence reminded Lewis of ... death.

The emptiness didn't help much, either. The space ran on forever, it seemed, with no carpets or furniture to cheer things up, and there was no one to be seen ... Wait, there *was* someone way in the distance. And beside this person was a massive desk, in front of which another person was seated, though Lewis couldn't make their details out. Without being told to, Lewis and his compatriots inched forward.

A minute later both figures were in focus. The person standing was Elizabeth Grumpel, dressed in the outfit Lewis had seen her in last, only it was zebra-striped now. She was rubbing her charm and had a wolf-like grin.

The seated figure was gaunt and very grim. His eyes were an unsettling shade of green — they looked like flashing Christmas bulbs — and his skin was milky white, as if it hadn't felt the sun in ages. His hair was grey, yet his face was unwrinkled, probably because he hadn't smiled in years. He was dressed in a black suit and, like Elizabeth, was wearing a charm around his neck. Beside him was a globe of the world — it was eight feet tall and remarkably detailed, with plastic reconstructions of cities, lakes, and mountains.

On his desk stood a block of gold engraved with fancy lettering: ERNST K. GRUMPEL. There he was, the great man himself, billionaire, bully, and chemical genius.

Murderer, too, Lewis was thinking, and it took all his strength to keep his anger in check.

"Look who's here," Elizabeth sneered. "And I see you brought some friends along. Were you too chicken to come alone?"

"That will do," her father rumbled in a voice that was deep and emotionless. "Let's bid our guests welcome. Allow me to introduce myself. I am Ernst K. Grumpel, the head of Grumpel Chemicals. And you are Lewis Castorman," he added, nodding at Lewis and eyeing him closely. "You look the spitting image of your father."

"Where is my father?" Lewis demanded, standing in front of the desk. "And why did you attack us with sleeping gas?"

Elizabeth laughed. "My, we are irritable."

"Elizabeth, please," Grumpel called to his daughter. Then he said to Lewis, "I'll answer your questions, but first things first. Let's have a spot of breakfast, shall we?"

Grumpel pressed a button on his desk. A nearby part of the floor rolled open and a platform appeared, bearing a table and five chairs. In addition to five settings, there was a platter with a dome and three porcelain jugs. Lewis heard his stomach growl.

"Food!" Todrus murmured. "What a good idea!"

As they sat at the table, Elizabeth took the dome off the platter. Expecting a feast, the group groaned in disappointment. The platter was piled with newspaper scraps, while the jugs contained nothing but water.

"That's a mean trick to play," Alfonse muttered.

"After kidnapping us," Adelaide spoke, "the least you could do —"

Elizabeth held up a three-inch vial that was fitted with an atomizer and held a bubbling liquid. With a bored look she sprayed the newspaper scraps and the water in the jugs. She then retreated from the table and reached for her charm.

Seconds later the scraps started smoking. Without warning there was an ear-splitting pop and the platter was covered with a solid, pinkish substance. It looked like rubber but smelled … delicious. The jugs, too, were wafting steam, and a coffee-like fragrance filled the air.

"Breakfast is served," Grumpel announced.

No one moved. The smells might be tempting, but this goop was nothing more than old newsprint.

"How bad can it be?" Alfonse finally asked, cutting off a corner of the pinkish substance.

"Well?" his friends asked, expecting him to gag.

Instead Alfonse cut himself a larger portion. "It's great! It's sweet and juicy and … help yourselves!"

The group began to dig in. Alfonse was right. The food was … interesting. It tasted a lot like scrambled eggs and provided everyone with a feeling of wellness.

As they ate, Grumpel explained how the vial's spray could transform any natural "base" — wood, earth, paper, stone — into an edible substance that was nutritious and tasty. He also said this single vial could prepare enough food to last a family for a year.

"All done?" Grumpel asked, once the group stopped eating. "In that case would you stand back from the table, please?"

As the group stood and retreated a few steps, Elizabeth took a second vial from her pocket and let a single, shiny drop spill out — it was like molten silver. As soon as this liquid touched the table, the plates, platters, jugs, and cutlery vanished in a puff of smoke. And with the click of a button the platform disappeared.

"Back to business," Lewis declared. "Where's my father?"

"Yes, yes, yes." Grumpel waved a hand dismissively. "Do you realize that, of all the locksmiths I tested, not one of them, besides your father, was as skilled as you?"

"Why do you need a locksmith?" Todrus asked.

"Why do you think? To open a lock! A complicated lock, I might add, a specialty job that took weeks to install. You've heard of Yellow Swamp?"

"I know all about Yellow Swamp!" Lewis cried, unable to control his temper any longer. "You destroyed the region and killed my mother in the process!"

"Goodness me!" Grumpel said. "Do you have any evidence to support this theory? If you're going to make such wild accusations, you should be able to prove them at least."

"I have witnesses!" Lewis hollered, forgetting to be cautious. "My friends saw your henchmen dump some stuff into the swamp. They also watched my mother die."

"Are you referring," the chemist purred, "to those frogs by your side? If so, who would take their word over mine?"

"How did he know?" Gibiwink asked, while Todrus glanced in Adelaide's direction.

"Are you really frogs?" she asked in a slightly strangled tone.

"We are," Todrus admitted, lifting his moustache for an instant.

Adelaide flinched. "What happened? I mean, how —"

"That's my doing!" Grumpel roared. "I gave them intelligence and I can take it away. Yes, Lewis Castorman, your mother's dead because of me," he added, "but I only acted to protect my secrets. Great deeds sometimes require the deaths of small people."

Lewis charged the desk. Grumpel merely smirked. Lifting a plain aerosol can, he sprayed it once, and a green cloud took shape. As soon as Lewis struck this gas, he was catapulted back as if shot from a cannon. If the frogs hadn't caught him, he would have flown fifty feet.

"Now listen closely," Grumpel said, pointing on his globe to northern Alberta. "Your mother constructed a lock in Yellow Swamp. A helicopter will fly you out to this region, where you'll find this lock and break it open. This task should be mere child's play for a locksmith of your calibre."

"But Yellow Swamp is closed," Todrus protested. "The area's too unstable."

"Never mind that!" Grumpel snarled. "I want that lock open and you will do as I say! And by this I mean *all* of you!"

"Forget it," Lewis said. "I refuse to help my mother's —"

Grumpel pressed a second button on his desk. The wall behind him clouded over and revealed a giant TV screen. A shadowy image gradually took shape: a man was lying in a sunken chamber, his arms and legs frozen solid. Three figures were poised above him, each armed with a gun. In the background the sound of dripping water could be heard.

"You asked about your father," Grumpel said. "I'm afraid he isn't well."

The angle changed, and the man's face filled the screen. Lewis's hair stood on end. This ragged figure was none other than his father. His face was pale and filthy, he had a straggly beard, and his clothes were in tatters. His father's shirt bore a bright orange stain, and Lewis understood why his limbs weren't moving — he had been hit with a Petriglobe.

"Dad!" he yelled. "Over here! It's Lewis!"

"I hired him to open the lock," Grumpel murmured, "but caught him snooping for proof that I killed your mother. Even now he refuses to help, and that's why you're here."

"Dad! Speak to me! Are you okay?"

"There's no point yelling," Elizabeth jeered. "He can't hear you."

"Let him go!" Lewis cried. "Let him go or I'll —"

"You'll do what you're told!" Elizabeth said sternly,

rubbing her charm more violently than ever. "You'll go to Yellow Swamp and then we'll free your stupid father. Otherwise he'll die, and you can be sure we won't use our *elixir vitae* —"

"Quiet!" Grumpel cried, touching the charm around his neck for an instant. He then added to Lewis, "Your father's life is in your hands."

Lewis stared at Grumpel. Although he was sick with worry about his father, he wondered how people could be so evil. Had Grumpel banged his head perhaps and dashed his conscience into a thousand pieces? Maybe he had been born an evil genius and there was nothing that would change this awful fact. Unless he had lost both his parents as a child and decided to take revenge on the world …

"If we do open that lock," Lewis finally said, "how do I know you'll release my father? I mean, afterward we might run to the police —"

Grumpel threw Lewis a terrible look. "Once the lock is open, you can run to the police and tell them anything you please. At that stage I won't care, believe me. Just do this job and I'll free your father and you can go back to your normal routines."

"But —"

"That's enough talk. You have your instructions. My daughter will take over from here." Grumpel turned away and stared at his globe.

"This way," Elizabeth said. With her charm between her fingers she led the group across the room. Off in the distance the door stood open and, barely visible, the guards were waiting. Wordlessly, the group followed in her wake. Only Lewis paused for a moment to take a final look at Grumpel.

The chemist was on his feet and embracing the globe. His head was thrown back in a posture of triumph, as if the entire world were his plaything now. The sight was … horrific. Lewis hurried after his friends, relieved to leave the evil genius to himself.

CHAPTER 7

It had been half an hour since they left Grumpel's office. The group was seated in a transport helicopter in immaculate white outfits and with packs around their waists. Elizabeth and twelve guards were stationed at the front, eyeing their prisoners with obvious scorn. The craft was barrelling through a pale blue sky, and New York City was just a speck in the distance.

Everyone was silent. They couldn't believe they were off to Alberta. Just that morning they had awakened in Mason Springs, and now they were up to their necks in danger.

Gibiwink flicked his tongue in and out. He and Todrus had cast their disguises aside and were dressed in white like everyone else. That meant they really looked like frogs, only ones that were a hundred times larger than normal. Adelaide studied them with open fascination.

For his part Lewis was dwelling on his father. With his limbs frozen in that prison of his, he had seemed so thin and vulnerable. How long could he last?

"Attention!" Elizabeth shouted. She was in the aisle rubbing her charm as usual. "It's time I explained your supply belts to you."

Alfonse glared at her. "Never mind the belts! I hate

these outfits and want my old clothes back."

"Your tie and jacket were stupid," she said. "More to the point, these outfits have been treated. They'll regulate your temperature, whether it's hot or cold outside. They'll also keep your bodies clean and bandage minor wounds."

"Very clever," Lewis said. "What's inside these belts?"

Elizabeth yawned. "You can open them. But be careful with their contents."

Curious, the group worked their waist packs open. Inside they found a series of compartments, each bearing a letter from *A* to *Z*. Unzipping one compartment, Lewis spied a row of vials — some holding pills, others containing finely ground powders, and still others filled with liquids of varying colours. Each vial was carefully labelled with words that were long and hard to pronounce. There was also a manual thick with instructions.

"The number one item," Elizabeth went on, "is your food transformer. You'll find it in your pack's front pocket. That's it," she added as Lewis took out a vial like the one she had used at breakfast. "Spray it on anything and you'll never go hungry."

"And these?" Todrus asked, pointing to the vials in his belt.

"I won't go into details," Elizabeth drawled. "But if you're faced with an emergency, consult your booklet. It has 'recipes' you might find useful. Okay?"

"I don't know," Todrus said, inspecting a label that read PLECTALIENORITHAMIN. "I've never handled chemicals like —"

"I'm not a teacher!" she snapped. "Figure it out for yourself!"

She stormed off to the front of the craft. The friends closed their belts and tried to relax.

To distract himself from brooding on his father, Lewis studied the landscape below. The helicopter was flying over an endless lake. Twenty miles to their right was a cluster of buildings and, higher than the rest of them, a large concrete tower.

"Where are we?" Alfonse asked, squeezing his head beside Lewis.

"We're over Lake Ontario and crossing into Canada. On our right is Toronto — that structure you see is the CN Tower. My mother installed a Dunbar Module in Toronto's airport, the first of its kind in North America."

Alfonse whistled. "You really know your geography."

"My mother said Canada was my second home. That's why we were always travelling to Quebec, Ontario, Prince Edward Island, and Alberta. We even camped in Yellow Swamp the summer before that chemical spill."

"Why do you think Grumpel built that lock in Yellow Swamp?" Alfonse whispered so their captors couldn't hear.

For the next few minutes they discussed the possibilities. Alfonse argued he was safeguarding a treasure — diamonds, gold, that sort of thing. Lewis disagreed. Why would Grumpel store his loot in Alberta when a vault in New York City would serve just as well? And why would he make the region so unstable? And then there was that egg-shaped boulder the frogs had seen his henchmen drop. No, something else was at stake.

"Like what?"

"I don't know. Weapons maybe or something illegal …"

Their conversation faltered. Alfonse returned to his seat, while Lewis studied the land as it passed. He found it comforting to be in Canada again — it made him feel a little closer to his mother.

The helicopter was travelling at a terrific speed. In no time at all Lake Huron was below them, then Sault Ste. Marie and the sprawling mass of Lake Superior. After that there was a continuous mass of forest, lakes, and wilderness for as far as he could see.

Another city soon appeared on the horizon. Lewis guessed this must be Winnipeg. He remembered a souvenir his mother had given him once. It was a model of Winnipeg in a plastic bubble which, when shaken, created a whirlwind of mosquitoes. MOSQUITO CAPITAL OF THE WORLD was written on its base.

The memory stabbed him like a six-inch blade.

He wondered how it would feel to forget. If he could erase his memories of his mother, would he do it? They had spent such happy times together studying locks, reading books, camping out and going on picnics, but that was the problem, wasn't it? As joyful as those memories were, at the same time they triggered such a terrible longing, reminding him as they did that she was gone forever, that she would never show him her designs again, never thrill him with her songs, jokes, and laughter. He would be better off, wouldn't he, without those thoughts to remind him of the treasures he had lost? If he could delete those memories, he would do so in an instant.

Mercifully, he drifted off.

"Wake up!" Elizabeth called as a guard shook Lewis roughly.

Outside, the sun was nearing the horizon. The land below was flat and dusty. Here and there brown specks appeared, and Lewis assumed these were herds of cattle. They were flying over mid-eastern Alberta.

"We're heading north," Elizabeth said. "And should be there very soon."

"And then?" Todrus asked.

"We've discussed that already. You'll look for the swamp, find the lock, and complete your mission." She rubbed her charm. "Of course, it won't be easy."

Gibiwink yawned. "Why's that?"

"Our chemicals destroyed a wide area," she admitted, "and we're not sure where the original swamp's located. The one thing we know is that it's bleeding ion clusters — that's a harmless type of radiation — and we'll drop you where our sensors pick these up. The swamp itself is easily recognized."

"How?" Alfonse asked.

"You'll see a hill with two large crests. These sit in the middle of a blood-red lake. The lock lies at the foot of this formation."

There was a buzz on the intercom. The pilot announced they were nearing the Yellow Swamp region. Hearing this, everyone flocked to the windows.

Lewis felt his stomach churn. There, in the distance, a black mass screened the horizon, as if a dragon were disfiguring the sky with its breath. It wasn't like a normal bank of cloud, but looked permanent and ...

menacing. Anything could happen in a fog like that.

He scanned his friends' expressions. They were obviously thinking along similar lines — Gibiwink had wrapped his tongue around Adelaide's shoulders. Always a polite girl, she pretended not to notice.

"Challenging, isn't it?" Elizabeth asked, pulling a package from an overhead locker. "It's a good thing we brought these patches along."

"This fog covers a large area," Lewis marvelled.

"It's a hundred miles by a hundred miles," Elizabeth said, removing a stack of patches from the package. She peeled a strip off one of them and disclosed a sticky surface.

"Does it bother you," Lewis asked, "that your father ruined such a huge piece of land?"

"No," Elizabeth said evenly, slapping a patch onto his back. "Canada's enormous. So what if a tiny part of it's polluted? Besides, it's partially your mother's fault. She suggested we build the lock in Yellow Swamp. She knew we were looking for a secluded place and was convinced Yellow Swamp would fit the bill. Not that she knew we were going to transform it. Her one concern was to build an unbreakable lock."

Elizabeth's observation took Lewis aback. An unbreakable lock — that sounded like his mother. So her one great ambition had brought about her death. As he wrestled with a knot of sadness, Elizabeth slapped patches on everyone's back.

"What's this for?" Adelaide asked, examining the patch.

Before Elizabeth could answer, the helicopter

lurched forward. Gibiwink was hurled to the front of the craft and, because his tongue was around Adelaide still, he yanked her in his wake. Unfortunately, the pair bowled Alfonse over, who bashed into Lewis, who crashed into Todrus, who knocked Elizabeth into the henchmen.

"We've entered the fog," Elizabeth wheezed, pinned beneath Todrus's left flipper. "Frog! Let go! You're cutting off my breath!"

Slowly, everyone regained his or her feet. Moving to a window, Lewis glanced outside. There were black clouds around them forming a solid wall. If it was like this above, what was the land like below? How would they —

"My charm! It's gone!" Elizabeth wailed, feeling her neck frantically. "It must have fallen off when we were knocked together!"

Adelaide shrugged. "Your dad will replace it."

"That charm's unique!" Elizabeth cried. "Search around everyone! I want it back!"

A whistle intruded, and a light started flashing.

"Our sensors have picked up ion clusters," she said, biting her lower lip in frustration. "The charm will have to wait. You have to get to the swamp."

"You can't see anything," Todrus observed, a flipper in his pocket. "How are we going to land in this fog?"

"That's why I put those patches on," Elizabeth said. "They're filled with helium and —"

"Like Zapper Dash!" Alfonse cried. "He wears an outfit that lets him float on air!"

Elizabeth laughed, her tone uncharacteristically warm and friendly. "That's right, squirt. In fact," she added, steering him a few feet to her left, "how'd you like to fly like him?"

"That sounds okay ..." Alfonse said warily.

As he spoke, Elizabeth grabbed hold of a lever, the floor gave way, and Alfonse was pitched into the fog.

"Alfonse!" everyone yelled above a screaming wind.

"Who's next?" Elizabeth asked, standing by the hatch.

"That was cold-blooded murder!" Lewis shouted.

"Say your prayers!" Adelaide growled, advancing on the chemist's daughter.

Elizabeth chuckled. "Relax. Landing in this fog is out of the question, and that means all of you have to jump. If I'd warned you in advance, you might have chickened out. Whereas now —"

"He'll die!" Lewis fumed. "He hasn't any parachute!"

Elizabeth smirked. "A parachute requires skill, while the Heliform patch lets you coast like a feather. Now let's get moving!"

"How do we communicate?" Todrus asked. "Are you giving us a radio?"

"They won't work in this region," Elizabeth said. "As soon as you jump, you're on your own. But you'd better hurry. Your friend is waiting ..."

"All right," Lewis said, nearing the hole in the floor. "But when all of this is —"

He didn't finish. The craft lurched wildly and toppled him outside. "Lewis!" he heard his friends cry out until their voices were drowned in the encompassing fog. He fell like a brick for a couple of seconds and was just about to yell in terror when the helium in his patch kicked in. As Elizabeth had promised, it slowed his fall.

Lewis looked around him. Every so often a cloud erupted and waves of gas crashed against him, causing him to cough or hold a hand to his nose. The patterns formed were spectacular: blues, reds, and yellows jumped forward, then receded quickly like beads in a kaleidoscope.

After several minutes, the clouds parted abruptly. One moment he was swimming in a storm of black cotton, the next he was tumbling through an iron-grey sky. He was a thousand feet above the earth ... or what was left of it at least.

The devastation was awful. Where there should have been trees, meadows, and streams, there was nothing but a sea of mud and steaming geysers. It stretched as far as the eye could see — drab, hideous, bleak, and lifeless, its surface swaying back and forth at the touch of each breeze. Had he really camped in this region once?

Then he spied something big hurtling skyward like a missile. It looked like a boulder. Yes, that was what it was — a mass of stone the size of a truck. It was muscling straight toward him. It was a hundred feet away, eighty, sixty ... Flecks of mud spun off its surface. With a cry of panic Lewis twisted right as the rock rushed forward to crush him like an insect!

Whoosh! It missed him by a couple of feet, and the backdraft twisted him head over heels. The mass then **gradually** came to a stop, plunged back down, and punched a hole in the chaos.

Lewis continued his descent. He wanted desperately to stay afloat — the ground was one vast puddle of mud — but gravity had other ideas. Moments later he crashed into the earth.

He sank fifteen feet. The mud was heavy and sucked him downward. He thrashed and kicked and splashed, but to no avail. Just as his lungs were beginning to burn, again the Heliform came to the rescue. Like a giant hand, it dragged him to the surface. Even as he gulped in mouthfuls of air, he heard a cry from somewhere in the distance.

"Lewis! Over here!"

"Alfonse!" he coughed back.

"Let's swim to each other! We'll meet halfway!"

For the next few minutes they swam together, shouting to keep each other on track. Both smiled with relief when they came face to face.

"Are you okay?" Lewis asked.

"I am now. For a while I was scared I'd be stuck here on my own. And you?"

"I'm fine, though I could use a shower. But over there! That's Adelaide falling!"

"That's her all right. This place is bad enough without her tagging along."

"Let's call to her. That way she can steer her way over."

"Are you sure? Imagine if she got lost in this mud ..."

"Alfonse! Quickly, while she's still falling!"

The two of them shouted and caught her attention. By twisting her arms and legs in mid-air, she was able to steer herself roughly above them. A minute later she was floating beside them, coughing and gasping from her bath in the mud.

They repeated the process for Gibiwink and Todrus, who had jumped together and were clutching each other. Once the frogs were bobbing beside them, their circle was complete.

"What now?" Gibiwink asked.

"Those ion clusters mean we're close to the swamp," Lewis said.

"I'm afraid," Todrus moaned. "We're nowhere near it."

"They dropped us in the wrong place," Gibiwink agreed.

Lewis craned his neck and surveyed their surroundings. For miles and miles in every direction there was nothing but mud to greet the eye. Certainly, there was no sign of any two-crested mountain. And in the distance, beyond the tar-coloured clouds, he could hear the rumble of the helicopter receding.

He nodded grimly. The chances of returning home were one in a million.

CHAPTER 8

W*homp!*
"That makes it an even fifty," Todrus said.

"Fifty-one," Gibiwink corrected him.

"I'm telling you, it's fifty," Todrus insisted.

"You'd be able to keep count," Alfonse said, "if my sister stopped singing."

"My singing keeps my spirits up."

"But it's driving us crazy!"

Lewis sighed. Everyone was grumpy. They had been swimming aimlessly for hours on end, and still they were up to their necks in mud. At the same time the sky was a mass of grey, the land was shaking like a bowl of jelly, and the wind was blowing from every side at once, creating waves of mud that kept pitching them over. While the Heliform patches were helping them float, they were tired of paddling and wiping muck from their eyes.

Whomp!

"Fifty-two."

"That's fifty-one, you nincompoop!"

The worst part was the boulders. Every so often there was a loud explosion and an elephant-size stone rose a mile upward, only to crash down and roll a wave toward them. Three times they were scattered like pins in a bowling alley.

"This mud won't end," Gibiwink whined. "And we're swimming in circles."

"And that darkening mass means trouble," Lewis muttered, nodding to a purple haze on the horizon. "Something strange is headed this way."

"Things look grim," Todrus agreed. "But at least they can't get worse … Arrgh!"

His cry of surprise made everyone flinch, especially when he leaped from the water.

"Something touched me," he explained moments later. "I'm sure it's nothing dangerous, but I'll dive and check it out."

That said, he did a backward flip and plunged beneath the surface. Lewis expected him to be gone for a minute, but he returned seconds later, looking pale and nervous.

"Things are worse than I imagined," he said. "There are hundreds and hundreds of leeches below, the smallest of which is three feet long."

"Leeches!" everyone cried in horror.

"Swim close together!" Lewis shouted. "And keep your voices down so we don't attract their notice. Maybe they'll lose interest and swim —"

Even as he spoke, something slimy touched his foot. At the same time a shape emerged from the water — black and long and tubular, with suckers attached to a rubber-like belly. The suckers were pointed straight at Lewis. When the creature launched itself at him, he punched it without thinking. His fist sunk into the beast's body, and a sticky fluid oozed around it. Much to his relief the creature returned to the depths, only to be replaced by a thousand others. Rising together, they lifted the group from the water — it was as if an island was taking shape beneath them.

"This isn't so bad," Gibiwink whispered. "At least we're getting a bit of a rest."

"Maybe these creatures are trying to help," Todrus said.

"The Bombardier was once surrounded by fish," Alfonse muttered. "They were friendly at first until they tried to eat him."

"Shut up about your comics!" Adelaide screeched. "Mention them again and I'll —"

Adelaide's threat ended in a cry of pain. Her calf was bare, and a leech had stabbed it. Quick as a flash, she kicked it away, but not before a cloud of blood took shape. Its smell and taste drove the creatures crazy. The horde began to quake all over, pitching Lewis and his friends to their knees as if they were standing on a large mound of jelly.

Two suckers cut into Lewis at once, one in his hand, the other near his ankle. Even as he drew them out, a couple more assaulted him. They couldn't penetrate his outfit, true, but attacked him where his flesh was exposed, or wherever they could worm into his clothing. He shrugged these off, then another half-dozen, punching and kicking as fast as he could. Adelaide and Alfonse were fighting just as madly, and bleeding from at least five different wounds.

It was lucky the leeches weren't interested in frogs. Their skin was much too thick for the leeches' suckers, and this left them free to attack the brutes. Again and again they hammered out, bruising them, denting them, and ripping off their suckers. At one point they lifted thirty leeches at once — the ooze from the creatures' wounds had them stuck together — and heaved them fifty feet into the air.

Stunned and frightened, the mass retreated.

"They've backed off!" Lewis cried, blood trickling from his outfit.

"They'll attack again," Todrus panted. "The smell of your blood is just too tempting."

"It isn't fair," Gibiwink complained. "For every one I smash a hundred others show up."

"And look at the sky," Alfonse moaned. "It's about to explode!"

It was true. While they had been fighting, the distant haze had taken over the sky. The air was heavy and crackling unpredictably.

"I suspect," Todrus mused, "we're in for a Zilatsky effect."

"What's a Zilatsky effect?" the others asked.

"It's the inversion of the soil's igneous compounds and —"

Before he could finish the chemistry lecture, a bolt of lightning jumped alive, but not like any lightning Lewis had seen. Instead it was more like molten metal, and when it smashed into the mud, a mile or two off, it triggered a change in the soil's texture. A band of yellow sped toward them.

"We're going to be electrocuted!" Gibiwink wailed.

"Not if the leeches kill us first!" Lewis cried.

The leeches. They were charging again. Their thrashing was causing the water to boil, and the surface was quivering with suckers past counting. Lewis heard Adelaide scream — unless that shriek had come from him.

Again the leeches raised them out of the water, and the children flinched as twenty suckers struck at once. Lewis kept punching, but his attackers were too many. His legs and stomach and back were hit, and he could feel the blood literally being sucked from his body.

One leech in particular — it was over six feet long — scrabbled over the roiling masses and aimed itself at Lewis. Pinning him, it assailed his throat with its suckers.

Lewis struggled hard, but the leech was slurping all over.

It was exactly then that the yellow band struck. There was a blinding flash, the air split apart, and the leech went flying as if yanked by an invisible hand. The suckers, thank goodness, had disappeared …

But wait! The mud had turned a bright yellow! And what … how? It was hard as stone! The leeches were trapped beneath its surface, and here and there the odd sucker protruded.

Lewis wheeled to inspect his surroundings. He couldn't budge. The mud had hardened around his feet and calves, his elbows, wrists, and the back of his skull — the parts of him, in other words, that had been touching the mud when it froze over.

"Is everyone okay?" Lewis yelled, alarmed that someone's head might be buried in the substance. When his friends answered yes but that their limbs were pinned, he asked if anyone knew what had happened.

"It was the Zilatsky effect," Todrus said. "It carbonized the sediment and —"

"Forget your science!" Gibiwink interjected. "How do we escape this mess?"

Lewis strained against the soil, searching out a pressure point, twisting back and forth and slackening his muscles in an effort to lessen the grip on his limbs. He tried this manoeuvre a dozen times, but the hardened mud refused to relinquish its hold.

"I'm afraid this mud's unbreakable," he groaned. "I'm sorry. I should never have let you come on this mission."

"It's not your fault," Todrus said. "Gibiwink and I volunteered, remember?"

"I did, too," Alfonse added. "And my sister wouldn't take no for an answer."

Adelaide glared at her brother. "I had a recital! I wanted to practise! Do you think I would have hitched a ride if I'd known I'd end up dying like this?"

"I told you not to come!" Alfonse snapped, "For once you should have listened to me!"

The pair started shouting in earnest, and Lewis wished he could block his ears. Before he and Alfonse had become best buddies, he had always wanted a brother or sister, a family member in addition to his parents. After hearing the Pangettis squabble all these years, he thanked his lucky stars that he had no siblings.

They were back to their old grievances. Adelaide was yelling she was sick of his comics, and Alfonse was insulting her playing again. Lewis was about to intervene, but before he could an odour broke out.

"What's that smell?" Adelaide asked, pausing in mid-insult. "Is something burning?"

Alfonse wrinkled his nose. "The ground's heating up!"

"Todrus, is this part of the Zilatsky effect?" Lewis asked.

"No," the frog answered. "You'd see brown-red flecks from the iron sulfates."

"I'm causing the reaction," a soft, almost unearthly voice intruded. "Any moment now and you'll be free of this mud."

Everyone gasped and tried glancing round, but this person was standing outside their field of vision.

"Who's there?" Lewis demanded.

"I call myself the Stranger, Lewis."

"How do you know my name?"

"There's no time to explain. Please close your eyes. There will be a small explosion soon."

While they had been speaking, the mud's temperature had risen. It was also smoking violently now as bright green fumes that could have been sliced with a knife assailed their nostrils, choking them.

There was a flash of blue and a muted roar. The mud beneath the group broke apart, and their "bonds" dissolved into a hundred tiny fragments. After waiting for the shower of mud to clear, Lewis and his friends jumped to their feet.

A moment later they were confronting the Stranger. As hard as they tried to hide their reaction, one by one their jaws slackened in horror.

CHAPTER 9

The "Stranger" looked human, but there were a few crucial differences. Its limbs were misshapen and coated with a bark-like substance. Two ungainly humps grew out of its back, as well as three tentacles, each black and deadly-looking. A fourth was lying spent on the ground — it had been used somehow to break up the mud. Its feet consisted of two sprawling flippers, and while its head was roughly the size of a human's, it had no nose and one eye in its middle, a big, empty space with no pupil to speak of.

"Thanks for freeing us," Lewis said, concealing his disgust. "How did you —"

"Never mind," the creature replied, shy because of its hideous looks. "This mud will melt and the leeches will return. All of you must hurry to safety."

"But we're lost," Adelaide groaned. "We don't know where to go."

"I've been following you," the Stranger confessed. "And I know about your mission to Yellow Swamp. If you're willing, I can lead you there."

"Who *are* you?" Todrus demanded. "And why should we trust you?"

"There's no time to explain," the Stranger insisted, pointing to the ground whose surface was melting.

"You'll have to trust me. That's all there is to it."

Without further ado, the Stranger hurried off. As it moved, it dragged its feet against the soil and produced an ugly, slapping sound. For a moment the group hesitated, not knowing what to think of this monster. As the mud rose past their ankles, however, they nodded to one another and set off in its wake. If it wanted to hurt them, it would have done so already.

"Have you noticed something?" Adelaide asked a few minutes later. "None of us is bleeding."

"So?" Alfonse jeered.

"She's right," Lewis said, examining his limbs. "I was bleeding when we were fighting the leeches. Yet, as far as I can tell, my cuts are gone."

"It's these outfits," Todrus said. "They've bandaged your wounds. That Grumpel has come up with some terrific inventions."

"Let's test his other stuff," Alfonse recommended, "and fix ourselves a meal."

Everyone agreed, their stomachs rumbling. The last time they had eaten was in Grumpel's office, and they had burned a lot of energy since. Unfortunately, the Stranger wouldn't hear of resting — the mud was melting quickly and every second counted.

But they had to eat. Telling the others to continue marching, Lewis removed his food transformer, aimed it at the ground, and sprayed three times. *Pop!* The soil changed in front of his eyes. From mud it was transformed into a pinkish goop, hot to the touch and delicious-smelling. He gathered up a mound of it and chased after the others.

Todrus flicked his tongue. "This stuff is incredible." He bolted down a juicy hunk. "The reaction is part hydrokinesis and part enzyme transfer, if I'm not mistaken."

Gibiwink sighed. "Never mind the science. This goop is tasty!"

After eating a few mouthfuls, Adelaide ran forward and offered some to the Stranger. It was moving as fast as its webbed feet allowed and focusing hard on the path before them.

"You should eat something, too," she said, handing it the goop.

"Thank you," it replied. "That's very kind of you."

"How do you know where to go?" she asked. "Everything looks alike in this region."

"The swamp speaks to me. I'm following its voice."

"Oh."

Adelaide reported her exchange with the Stranger to the others. Everyone wondered how a swamp could speak, and again they had serious doubts about their guide.

Todrus, though, squeaked with excitement. "It makes sense. It's ion conductivity. The Stranger was present when Yellow Swamp blew up. It absorbed the ion clusters at large, and these are naturally drawn to the swamp, the same way iron is attracted to magnets."

"And that's why we landed so far from the swamp," Adelaide added. "The chopper picked up the Stranger's ion clusters and not ones coming from the swamp itself."

They continued forward. At one point the question arose why Grumpel had decided to ruin this landscape. Lewis said the spill had likely been an accident, that

Grumpel had maybe intended something smaller and not realized the effects would alter the region. The frogs disagreed: Grumpel didn't make mistakes, not when something huge was at stake. The damage was intentional, in other words. Adelaide, for her part, kept watching the soil, worried it would melt at any moment, while Alfonse said that in *Bombardier 19* Dr. Gong breeds dinosaurs in the Arctic region and changes the climate to keep them alive …

Everyone ignored him — a pity as it turned out.

Adelaide spotted the wall of haze first, about a mile in the distance. "Excuse me," she called out. "What's that cloud up ahead?"

"It's the Pother," the Stranger said, breaking off its concentration. "Did I mention it was dangerous?"

The group moaned. "Dangerous?"

"Lethal," the Stranger declared.

Lewis studied the obstruction. "How close will we go to it?"

"We'll be walking right through it," the Stranger told him. "And we'll be lucky to escape without someone disappearing. I just hope we reach it before the mud gives way."

The group looked down. By now the mud was up to their calves. If they didn't make it to the Pother soon, they would be bobbing in the muck again with the leeches in pursuit.

Some twenty minutes passed. Their legs were aching and they wanted to rest, but the mud was rising with each passing second. By now its depths had liquefied, too, and a mass of leeches was swimming beneath them. Only a foot of frozen mud stopped them from attacking. And to add to their troubles, the Pother towered above them.

It wasn't normal. Neither solid, gas, or liquid — nor animal, mineral, or vegetable, for that matter — it rose from the ground straight into the heavens and stood before them like a mountain range. Never mind its size (it overcrowded the sky), never mind its colour (it was like a blanked-out rainbow), and never mind the sounds it made (it was silent and deafening at the same time) — these features weren't as worrying as its projection of … futility. The more its outline came into focus, the more it seemed that nothing mattered, that laughter, tears, victory, failure, love, and hate were all the same, life and death, as well … life and death especially.

"I don't like this," Adelaide whispered.

"It smells of … nothing," Alfonse observed.

"My guess is," Todrus mused, "its atoms have been involuted."

"Is 'involuted' a real word?" Gibiwink snapped.

"Of course it is," Todrus insisted. "It means the collapse of matter as we know it, like a bag that isn't a bag but the empty space inside it."

"A bag of what?" Gibiwink demanded.

Before Todrus could answer, the Stranger drew them to a halt.

By now they were fifty yards away from the Pother. Unlike the usual bank of mist, which was there one moment and gone the next, the Pother was like a barrier … no, actually, like an open gate. Lewis stared into its depths. As hard as he strained, he couldn't make out its interior, couldn't see any trees or grass or anything. The roots of his hair tingled like crazy, as if they were hooked up to an electrical socket.

"We'll need a rope," the Stranger announced. "One long enough to bind us together."

"We didn't bring one," Lewis answered. "Can we just hold hands?"

"We need a rope," the Stranger repeated, "with knots that will hold no matter what. If one of us slips for even an instant, he'll never come back. And I mean never."

"Let's search our manuals," Adelaide suggested as the group shivered at the Stranger's words. Opening her belt, she took her booklet out. "Let's see. Refrigeration, relaxation, remembering," she read aloud from the index. "Ribbon, riches, here we go, rope. We'll need a drop of polyalienamethylene, a pinch of alienamoxocin, and a pentalienachlorophyll pill."

"Here they are," Alfonse and Lewis said, producing three vials between them.

"You need to hurry," the Stranger advised. "The mud is getting thin."

Their guide was right. The mud reached past their thighs. The frozen layer was only six inches thick, and below it the leeches were massing together. Some were battering the barrier to break it up faster.

"Let's make that rope quickly!" Adelaide said with a shudder.

They mixed the chemicals in with some mud. Seconds later there was a puff of smoke and a pool of liquid plastic appeared. When Adelaide pinched this substance and tugged it slightly, it started stretching like mozzarella cheese. She shaped a circle with her thumb and index finger and pulled the plastic through it as she tugged it further. It was forced into a tubular shape and, stretching three yards, five yards, ten, began to resemble a makeshift rope. By the time she produced thirty yards of the stuff, the material had stiffened into something like nylon.

"It's strong," Todrus said, testing the substance. "And as good as any rope I've seen."

"Then let's use it!" Alfonse cried, eyeing the leeches below.

"Can anyone tie knots?" Adelaide asked, flinching as a leech rammed the mud beneath her.

Lewis grasped the rope. He had learned to tie knots from an early age, understanding they weren't all that different from locks. That was why he arranged the group in a line, separating everyone by six feet. He then looped the rope about their waists and secured it with a "lobster pinch" — the strongest knot in existence. Within minutes they were fastened to one another. A good thing, too, since the mud was cracking up.

"They're breaking through!" Adelaide shrieked as a leech smashed the surface and scrabbled with its suckers.

"Follow me!" the Stranger cried. "And just keep moving, *no matter what*!"

Wading through the mud, it crossed into the Pother. Todrus followed, then the Pangettis, Lewis, and a nervous Gibiwink.

They heard the mud dissolve behind them. A mass of leeches flew into the air, slurping, burping, and stabbing with their suckers. Lewis felt one of them graze his neck. When another three lunged, he threw himself forward.

The Pother absorbed him as the ground gave way and with a gasp of fury the leeches vanished.

Caught inside the Pother, Lewis glanced around him. Whatever the substance was — mist, gas, vapours, shadow — it was impossible to stare into, however hard he peered. His friends were invisible, as were his arms and legs — he couldn't spot his fingers when he held them to his eyes. This wouldn't have been shocking had the Pother been black, but it was white, bright, bedazzling, in fact, as if he were standing at the heart of a light bulb.

"Alfonse!" he called out. "Isn't this weird?" He received no answer but was bombarded with sound — "FONSE FONSE ISSSNNN THISSSS IIISS EEEEERRD!" The lesson was clear: within this Pother, they were on their own.

Falling silent, he "followed" the rope. Because the ground was invisible, walking wasn't easy. He closed his eyes, but that didn't help. And when something brushed against his leg — it was probably Alfonse who had stumbled briefly — he yelled in alarm, the sensation was so strange.

He counted a thousand steps. That done, he counted a thousand more, not just once but ten times over. Lewis was tired, and his legs, if they existed still, were sore. He hoped to reach their destination soon unless — the thought struck him — he had broken loose of the others and was wandering stupidly about on his own. The idea was so frightening that he started to panic until the rope reminded him he was joined to his friends.

No sooner had his panic waned than he felt the presence of something else. Not his friends, that would have been fine, but something odd and … hair-raising.

It was calling his name in a ghostly voice. "Lewis Castorman, Lewis Castorman!" There! A shadow was taking shape, like a vault of some type … it was an XPJ! Lewis tried to work it open — he could see its parts and move them at will. Yes, the tumblers were rolling and the bolts were slipping back. The door was opening and … what was that?

A human head stared back at him.

He strained his eyes. The head belonged to … his father!

"Dad, are you okay?" he whispered.

"DAADAADDDAADDD…YERYERYERYERYER … OHOHOHKAYKAYKAY" came booming back as the head began to fall apart, losing its eyes, ears, nose, and hair until nothing remained except a grinning skull. A second skull appeared, then another, and another, until he was surrounded by a crowd of them, their sockets black, their smiles blood-curdling. One skull bore the face of Ernst Grumpel! Its mouth yawned open and sprayed a chemical cloud.

Lewis missed his footing and hit the ground. *Aha!* So he was solid still! And his friends were near. These thoughts chased the phantom skulls away.

What were they? A mirage? And would they return? Lewis couldn't bear to see them again — they had been horrible, grinning in a vault like that. His worries mounted.

Wait! Was the Pother thinning? No doubt about it,

it wasn't as empty and, there, he could see someone's outline ahead.

"You can relax," the Stranger said. "The worst is over."

"Lewis," Alfonse murmured, "can you hear me?"

"Sure."

"This will sound pretty weird, but I saw The Bombardier. I could have touched him he was standing so close."

"I know what you mean."

"But he tried to kill me," Alfonse gasped. "He bared these fangs and complained I read too many comics."

"I saw Beethoven," Adelaide told them. "He said my playing is an insult to his genius."

Lewis nodded. The Pother toyed with people's thoughts, creating fear in place of pleasure. The worst part was that it divided its victims. Suffering was bad enough, but the worst thing was to face it alone.

"I'm glad you're here," he said to his friends.

They nodded back, too tired to speak.

The Pother was on its last gasp now. It was yellowing at its edges and spiralling off. With a final *whoosh*, it ended abruptly as they entered a landscape that exploded with colour.

When they were finally free of the rope, the group sank to the ground.

CHAPTER 10

After resting for fifteen minutes to ease their tired muscles, Lewis and the others surveyed their surroundings. Although the sky was still a continuous grey, with no clouds, stars, or sun to break its finish, the landscape was much more cheerful in appearance. The hardened yellow mud was gone, and in its place was an expanse of emerald grass. Long stretches of it resembled a well-kept lawn, but here and there lay patches that were taller than the frogs. Back and forth its lush stalks swayed, like waves at the seaside when the wind blew.

There were flowers, too. These were huge and brilliantly coloured — their yellows, reds, and blues were brighter than fresh paint. And their fumes were so strong when smelled up close that Adelaide almost fainted when she tested a rose.

There was moss, as well — it made the perfect bed — and ferns that were big enough to use as ladders. This lushness was an improvement over the mud and Pother.

"This is amazing," Adelaide gasped, recovering from the rose's fumes.

"The grass is lovely," Gibiwink agreed. "And look at those ferns!"

"I'd be careful," Alfonse cautioned. "The Bombardier travels through a beautiful landscape, and that's when the Zagradorf just about kills him."

Adelaide was about to insult him when the ground started shaking.

There was a disturbance on their right in a distant patch of grass. The moss, ferns, and flowers began trembling, and bits of debris filled the air. There was also a discordant sound in the background as if a hundred radios were playing high-pitched noises at once. As the ruckus drew closer, the friends grew more anxious.

"I don't like this!" Todrus cried. "Let's find a hiding place!"

Behind them was a stretch of giant stalks, and the group plunged into the thick of them. A good thing, too — as soon as they had concealed themselves, the commotion spilled into the clearing.

They gasped. Before them stood an army of ants. These weren't the little insects that overran picnics. Each was almost the size of a car and armed with mandibles that looked like garden shears. If a plant blocked their path, they cut it to pieces.

"Don't move," the Stranger whispered. "Those are wood ants, and they're very aggressive. If they detect our presence, they'll swarm us for sure."

Everyone froze at the creature's words and listened closely as the ants drew near. The trampling of the grass grew unbearably loud and the high-pitched garble more and more frenzied. Through an opening in the stalks Lewis studied the army. He shivered. With its oversized legs, antennae, and thorax, each ant resembled a miniature tank.

For two long minutes the ants plodded by — dozens, maybe hundreds. Lewis kept waiting for a scout to appear and lead its companions to attack the intruders. At one point he *did* feel something sticky on his neck and spun around with his fists upraised. It was Gibiwink's tongue.

The last ant passed. Lewis was going to step into the open, but the Stranger held him back.

"There's no point," their guide whispered. "Not just yet. We're heading in the same direction as these ants. Let's give them some distance and in the meantime rest."

Everyone agreed. And because they were hungry, the frogs plucked a few stalks — these were maybe eight feet high — and crumpled them together. Alfonse sprayed them with his food transformer and changed the tangle into strands of pinkish goop.

The group ate with gusto, convinced the goop was tastier than ever.

The Stranger alone refrained. Again it was conscious of its odd appearance and too embarrassed to eat in front of the others. When Adelaide saw it was holding back, she placed a mass of goop in its lap. At the same time she inquired about its history.

"I can't remember much," it sighed, nibbling the food. "I was in Yellow Swamp when a cloud appeared. The water started boiling, and I seemed to be drowning. The next thing I knew, I was running away. 'Who are you?' I kept asking myself, but my memories were gone. At one point I paused to drink from a stream, and that's when I noticed my awful appearance. These tentacles, this skin, these hideous features — they filled me with disgust and I wanted to hide. Since that time I've remained in this region because I don't belong in the outside world."

The creature fell silent and stared at its food.

"We experienced the same confusion," Todrus admitted, giving the Stranger a pat with his flipper. "Like you, we were simple beasts that were suddenly able to think like humans."

"But you know what you are," the Stranger wailed. "Whereas I know nothing about my past. Apart from a poem, my memory is a blank."

"A poem?" Gibiwink asked, goop dripping from his snout. "Can you recite it, please? I love poetry."

"I don't know …" the Stranger said, hesitating. But Gibiwink kept pleading and the others joined in. With a sigh the creature began to recite.

> "I have no walls, no chains, no bars
> My prisoner's free to view the stars
> Yet move or be moved that cannot be,
> Unless you find the appropriate key.
>
> Three ingredients must be mixed as one
> The first a pale blue precious stone
> Hidden in the earth away from sight
> Its glow most generously enkindles light
>
> On its own this blue stone won't avail
> To release the treasure from my jail
> Unless joined with forgetful daffodil
> With petals pink and scent of caramel."

"There are other verses, too," the Stranger said, "but they've slipped my memory."

"But not mine," Todrus announced. Closing his eyes, he finished the poem.

> "In addition there is substance three
> A weed, yellow tipped, that embraces a tree
> The tree grows higher than all its brethren
> And upraises the weed toward the heavens
>
> Find me, determine my lowest point
> And upon my means of escape anoint
> The ingredients three, mixed into one
> And then my prisoner shall be won."

"Very interesting," Lewis observed once he and the others had finished applauding. "The question is, where did both of you hear it?"

"I couldn't say," the Stranger mused. "It's in my head. That's all I can tell you."

"I know," Todrus said with some reluctance. "Do you remember when we told you, Lewis, how your mother loved to sing while she worked? Well, that poem you heard was one of her songs."

"That's right!" Gibiwink burst out. "I knew it sounded familiar!"

"The Stranger lived in the swamp," Todrus added. "And like us it must have overheard your mother sing."

Lewis wasn't listening. He was remembering how, when his mother was alive, he had awoken each morning, not to the radio's jingles, but to her constant singing in the kitchen downstairs as she had fixed breakfast for him and his father. The early-morning warbler, his father had called her. At the time he hadn't thought much of her singing, but in the weeks and months that had followed her death, more than anything else he had missed her cheerful, sunny tunes.

He also recalled something else. His mother had once shown him an Ambassador lock, and when he had some trouble with its operation, she had composed a song to help him pick it open. "Eight pins on the spinner / pick them you're a winner" — those had been the first two lines. The point was her songs had had a purpose, had been designed to remind —

"Look at this!" Adelaide interjected. For the past few minutes she had been leafing through her instruction booklet. "There's a brew that lets you see into the immediate future!"

Her announcement came as such a surprise that the group ignored the poem for the moment and crowded around to find out more about this potion. Already Adelaide was taking vials from her belt — iodidalienacalcidite, alienoxenophine, a milligram of nealienahydroxide — and pouring their contents onto a stalk of grass. A cloud of grey-black smoke erupted, together with a ghastly smell — like gasoline and tomato juice mixed together.

"You're not going to eat that," Alfonse said, motioning to a tar-like substance.

"Why not?" Adelaide asked. "I've always wanted to see the future."

"I don't know," Lewis cautioned her. "There are some things we should leave alone."

"The Bombardier is exposed to radiation," Alfonse mused, ignoring his sister's look of irritation, "and suddenly he can tell the future. He reaches the same conclusion as Lewis — that we're better off not knowing what the future holds."

Adelaide laughed. "All the more reason to eat it. Anything The Bombardier hates is well worth trying." Upon saying that, she swallowed part of the tar.

Everyone watched with bated breath, expecting her face to swell and her skin to change colour. A minute passed, but nothing happened. Then suddenly she began to shriek. "We're about to be attacked!"

"What do you mean?" Alfonse said. "We're hidden in this grass."

"He's right," the Stranger reassured her. "We're well protected —"

"In a moment," Adelaide groaned, "Lewis will suggest we scout things out, Gibiwink will spill some goop on Todrus, and —"

"Maybe we should scout around," Lewis recommended.

"I'll go," Gibiwink volunteered, only to stumble as he tried to stand. Sure enough, a glob of goop splashed onto Todrus.

"Be careful with that stuff!" Todrus clucked, but his words were lost in the chaos that followed. From every side at once the giant grass was collapsing. Even as Lewis climbed to his feet, a wall of shadows burst around him.

Within seconds the entire group was down for the count.

CHAPTER 11

When Lewis finally came to, he couldn't get his bearings. He was stretched out and riding on some type of conveyance. He felt rested and that meant he had been out cold for a while. But his hands were tied, it was dark around him, and ... where was he? Who had captured him? And what about his friends?

"Hey!" he cried out.

There was silence, followed by high-pitched gibbering. He should have known. The ants!

"Lewis?" Alfonse whispered from nearby.

"Alfonse? Are you okay? What's going on?"

"We're underground," Todrus murmured. "Those ants we saw earlier must have snuck up from behind."

"And the others?" Lewis asked, probing his bonds with a pinky.

The rest of the group reported in and, apart from some bruises, were perfectly fine. The Stranger warned they might not be so lucky in the future.

"Don't mention the future," Adelaide groaned. "I never want to see it again."

Assured his friends were safe, Lewis worked on his bonds. The knot was a tough one — a double-loop crustacean — but feeling out the pressure points, he slackened its tension and slipped his wrists free. Groping around, he discovered he was on a makeshift stretcher that the ants had woven from the giant grass. It was supported by a series of ropes that in turn were tied to ...

"Ow!" Lewis yelped, grazing a razor-sharp surface. Angry noises revealed he had handled an ant's mandible and was lucky his fingers were still intact. He shared this information with the rest of the group.

"Where are we headed?" Gibiwink asked.

"To their nest," Todrus answered, "where there are probably another million ants like these."

"That's great," Adelaide fumed. "We're underground, surrounded by ants, tied up, and trapped in total darkness ..."

"Not quite total," Alfonse pointed out. "Do you see that blue glow up ahead?"

He was right. A few yards down a light was bleeding through the darkness. It came from a bluish stone embedded in the walls and ceiling. As they were carried forward and the glow embraced them, their eyes began to make sense of their surroundings.

"I preferred the dark," Adelaide moaned.

The others agreed. They were travelling through a rough-hewn passage that continued downward at a fairly steep angle. The passageway was narrow and made them feel claustrophobic. But the cramped space wasn't as bad as the ants. They numbered in the hundreds and filled most of the tunnel. Wherever the group happened to glance, antennae and mandibles greeted the eye. And the air was filled with an incessant gibbering that grated on the ears and sounded ... insulting.

"Is it me," Adelaide muttered, "or does this light seem familiar?"

"It's a form of desynapsis," Todrus explained. "There must be a mineral —"

"That's not what I mean," Adelaide snapped. "I'm referring to the poem the two of you recited. Wasn't there a line about a glowing stone?"

"'Hidden in the earth from sight / its kind blue glow enkindles light,'" the Stranger chanted.

"You see?" Adelaide said. "It's describing the stone around us."

"I guess," Gibiwink agreed. "But what does it mean?"

"How does the first bit go?" Adelaide prodded. "You know, that part about —"

"'I have no walls, no chains, no bars / My prisoner's free to view the stars,'" the Stranger sang.

"It sounds like the poem is describing a jail," Gibiwink ventured.

"That's it!" Lewis cried, remembering his train of thought before Adelaide had stumbled on the "future" potion. "That poem is an answer to some of our problems."

As the group listened closely, he explained how his mother's songs had contained clues for picking open her locks. That meant the song they had heard at Yellow Swamp was a formula for "cracking" the lock she had installed. So the *I* in the poem was the lock itself and its *key* was the three different objects she had mentioned — a blue stone, a daffodil, and a weed on a tree. Once these objects were applied to the lock, its mechanism would somehow come undone.

"So if we find these three objects —" Todrus began.

"*Two* objects," Adelaide interrupted, motioning with her chin to the rock in the walls. "We've already found the first of them."

"Two objects," Todrus agreed. "Then we can head to the swamp and the rest should be easy."

"That's assuming we survive these ants," Alfonse groaned.

The ants! By now they seemed to be nearing their goal. The way was blocked by two large boulders, and their guards were waving their antennae in excitement. The group could hear a raucous din ahead — it sounded like the shouts from a baseball stadium.

"I don't like this," Gibiwink whispered.

They approached the boulders. Between them was an opening wide enough to let the stretchers pass. The ants hauled them one by one through this crack, brushing each "passenger" with their six-foot antennae.

The light was almost blinding. It turned out there was so much of the blue stone present that it was casting enough light to outshine New York City. Once his eyes had adjusted to the glow, Lewis saw they were trapped in an underground cavern, one much bigger than an airplane hangar and with a ceiling that stood two hundred feet from the ground. Despite the cavern's size, the space seemed ... overcrowded.

Their escort was nothing like the hordes that greeted them. There were ants by the thousands, a whole city of them. They were arranged in lines that filled every inch of the cavern — like an invading army mustered for review. While their bodies were held at strict attention, their antennae jiggled back and forth, and Lewis felt seasick from this carpet of motion.

"This isn't good," Adelaide groaned.

Their guards stopped and set the stretchers down. They then stood their captives on their feet but didn't cut them loose. Because he had wriggled free of his bonds, Lewis searched his book for something helpful, being careful not to draw the guards' attention. He scanned the *B*s for *bug repellent*, the *S*s for *sprays*, the *F*s for *fumigation*. Nothing. In desperation he ransacked the *T*s for *trap*, *trance*, or *termination*. Then *traction*, *transformation*, *translation*, *transparent* ...

As he read, the ants opened a path in their ranks. It ran for maybe a hundred yards and ended against a pale blue boulder that was easily the size of a three-storey building and bathed the cavern in its turquoise brilliance. Half a dozen guards hustled the group forward, and as they navigated the path it closed behind them. Lines of ants were poised on every side, nosily grinding their mandibles together. The friends struggled to maintain their composure.

A minute later they were standing in front of the rock, which they could now see had been carved into a throne. Resting in its middle was the colony's queen.

She was ... elephantine. Her legs were maybe ten feet long, while her thorax and egg sac were the size of a truck. Her mandibles resembled a bulldozer's blades, and her eyes were like two TV screens, only black and empty and impossible to read. Strange to say, she seemed completely drained of energy.

An ant stood next to the throne, larger than the others but nothing like the queen. This figure flicked its antennae at the guards, who quickly snipped their prisoners loose. It then began to motion in the group's direction.

"It's trying to speak," Adelaide said. "I read somewhere that ants communicate this way."

"You're right," Todrus agreed. "And it wants us to answer." Sure enough, the ant repeated its gestures with what seemed to be impatience.

"I have an idea," Lewis said. Returning to the *T*s in his instruction book, he looked up *translation*, an entry he had spotted earlier. Lewis followed the recipe and selected vials of hydroxyalienisothene, nitroglyceridalienase, and aliendioxycide — the last of these was as black as licorice. As the ant signalled with mounting irritation, he hastily put the brew together, using his severed bonds as his "mixing base." The gesturing ant was getting angrier when the rope turned green. Without wasting time, Lewis bit into this mixture — it tasted like hot dogs with cantaloupe mixed in — and urged his friends to do the same.

The effect was instantaneous. One moment he was hearing unintelligible squeaks; the next he grasped their meaning perfectly, as if he had been listening to a radio's static and had finally tuned into an actual station. The others ate the rope, Gibiwink last of all.

"I am Thwashskaflr, adviser to the Shthaflr colony. What are your names? And why were you travelling through the giant grass?"

"Answer! Don't leave our adviser waiting!" the guards shouted. Beneath their anger, Lewis sensed a certain gloom, as if they were faced with an impending disaster.

114

What happened next surprised him. Without thinking twice, as if he had been doing it all his life, he began to gibber and motion with his fingers. "I am Lewis Castorman. I come from a distant nest called Mason Springs, and we are travelling through the grass to the swamp that is yellow."

"Greetings, Lewis from Mason Springs," Thwashkaflr answered. "Who are your companions? Let them identify themselves."

One by one they introduced themselves, and it was odd to see them "talking" with their fingers. Only Gibiwink couldn't make himself clear — by the time he had swallowed the last of the rope, most of the concoction had been eaten already. Instead of saying, "I'm Gibiwink from Yellow Swamp in Alberta," his words got twisted into, "The barnacle has cheese wings and cannot eat a pencil."

"Let us converse," Thwashkaflr gibbered with a puzzled look. "No doubt you wish to discover why we have led you here against your will."

"Your need must be great," Lewis said diplomatically.

"Indeed, you have spoken well. Our queen — may she flourish forever — has been stricken with an illness. While sound of thorax, she moves not, eats not, and lays no eggs. If her sickness lingers, our colony will die."

"What's this about toaster ovens?" Gibiwink whispered, misinterpreting the adviser's words.

"I'll explain to you later," Adelaide whispered back.

"As you observe," Thwashkaflr continued, "our nature has been altered. We are large and our faculties have been graced with understanding. After much thought, our counsellors determined our queen — may she flourish forever — is sick within her soul. In short, her majesty — may she flourish forever — suffers because she knows not laughter."

"Laughter?" Todrus repeated, taken aback.

"Laughter?" Lewis and the others echoed.

"Frying pans?" Gibiwink cried.

"Consequently," Thwashkaflr declared, "you must amuse our queen — may she flourish forever — so that she overcomes her sadness and yields us eggs again. A colony without eggs is no colony at all."

Alfonse chuckled. "Make the queen laugh? A piece of cake."

"But be warned," Thwashkaflr cried, her mandibles snapping. "Failure will lead to punishment. Our queen — may she flourish forever — will laugh, or you will suffer terribly!"

"Hey! That's not fair!" the group protested with a click of their heels.

A thousand ants took three steps forward. The friends fell silent and swallowed hard. The queen's inability to laugh was no laughing matter.

"We will begin immediately!" Thwashkaflr announced. "Who will be first?"

"There's no entry for laughing gas," Lewis whispered — again he had been reading his instruction book. "I hope one of us knows a few good jokes."

"Frogs aren't known for their sense of humour," Todrus groaned.

"Don't worry," Alfonse said. "I'll have the queen in stitches. Over here!" he called to Thwashkaflr. "Prepare yourselves for some great entertainment."

"I hope so for your sake," Thwashkaflr signalled, leading Alfonse forward.

"Good day, Your Majesty," Alfonse greeted, waving his fingers in front of the queen. "I'm here to tell you a couple of jokes. Why did the frog paint his flippers red?"

The queen showed no interest in this question.

"So he wouldn't be confused with a toad!" Alfonse answered.

"That's terrible," Todrus said.

"He's going to get us killed," Adelaide groaned.

"Why's he talking about propellers?" Gibiwink asked.

"I'm just warming up," Alfonse continued. "What's a frog's favourite song? Give up? 'A Froggy Day in London Town.'"

"It's not working," Todrus muttered, motioning to the queen who had turned her head toward the throne.

"Here's my favourite," Alfonse prattled on. "What's a frog's favourite soft drink? You want a hint? Croaka-cola!"

"Enough!" Thwashkaflr shouted as two guards dragged Alfonse back to his friends. "Your jokes aren't helping! Who's next?"

"I'll give it a shot," Todrus said. Moving forward, he signalled the queen, "Tell me please, Your Majesty, what's the difference between a steak and a TV set?"

"Does she know what a TV is?" Adelaide whispered.

"You can't barbecue a TV set!" Todrus cried with a bark of laughter.

The queen wasn't impressed.

"So tell me this, Your Highness," Todrus went

on, "what's the difference between a trumpet and a grand piano? You give up? You can't build a fire with a trumpet!"

The group, except Gibiwink, laughed. For her part the queen didn't stir.

"How about this?" Todrus babbled. "What's the difference between a Stradivarius and Havarti cheese? You can't use Havarti cheese as a doorstop!"

The group whooped with laughter, all but Gibiwink who was riffling through his manual. Unfortunately, the ants were unaffected. Thwashkaflr, in fact, was even angrier, and the guards hauled Todrus away from the queen.

"Next!" the adviser yelled by stamping her front legs against the ground.

Lewis then picked an imaginary lock, and Adelaide and the Stranger performed a comic sketch, in which they pretended to be adrift in the Pother. While their friends were almost crying with laughter, the ants betrayed no sign of amusement.

"Who's next?" Thwashkaflr roared. Signalling to Gibiwink, she yelled, "I see there's only one of you left. He better succeed or …"

"Gibiwink, concentrate!" Todrus implored, even as Thwashkaflr steered him to the queen. At the same time the ants stepped closer to their "guests" on the assumption they would be attacking them in a matter of seconds.

Now Gibiwink had long suspected there was something wrong with the translation brew. In fact, he was preparing himself a fresh batch when Thwashkaflr yanked him forward. That meant he couldn't talk to the queen — not intelligibly at least — and he couldn't close the vials that were open in his belt.

"Hello," he gibbered politely. "My name's Gibiwink, and it's nice to meet you." That was what he had intended to say. The queen and the ants had heard a different message, though: "Why are sausages blue? My carpet has a cough."

The queen turned her head from the throne, while the ants twitched their antennae in confusion, not knowing what to make of this nonsense.

"My translation brew is off," Gibiwink explained, "and that's why everything sounds so peculiar. If you'll give me a minute, I can mix a fresh batch."

The ants heard: "The window hates raisins. Do you eat toothpicks, too?"

"What's he doing?" Alfonse hissed. "Our lives are at stake!"

Lewis was too busy to answer. He was flipping through his book in search of a solution. There was a recipe for sleeping gas, but it would knock them out along with their aggressors. The same was true of the volcanic eruption, while the fire grenade seemed a little extreme. That left him with the smokescreen, but by now his motions had attracted the guards.

"Let go!" Lewis cried as they seized his arms.

"Hey! What's going on?" the others yelled as a cluster of guards assailed them, too. The message was clear: unless Gibiwink came through, all of them were doomed.

"I was never good at mixing things," the frog was saying. "Take cooking, for example. Every meal I prepare always comes out wrong, even toast and frozen waffles."

The ants heard: "The fork is hammering the napkin. My toenail is a suitcase."

"He's making them upset," the Stranger murmured.

That was true. The ants were breaking ranks and jostling one another to look at the frog who was sputtering such rubbish. The queen, too, had risen to her feet and was probing Gibiwink's face with her antennae.

"I'm afraid I don't know any jokes," the frog continued. "In fact, I'm not much good at anything. Todrus is clever and knows a lot of chemistry, while Lewis …"

The ants heard: "Your brain is weak. Give me melons, or I'll bite your moustache."

"That's done it," Adelaide whimpered. "Now they're really angry."

Lewis glanced up. The ants were grinding their mandibles together, and the queen was still probing Gibiwink and rubbing her antennae against his nostrils.

That was when the frog sneezed. The antennae tickled the inside of his nose, and he couldn't stop himself from letting loose. His sneeze was so powerful, in fact, that it hurled him back a couple of feet and caused his vials to mix their contents together.

There was a bright flash followed by a ball of smoke. A dark brown foam oozed from Gibiwink's belt and half buried the frog in popping bubbles — luckily, they had a chocolatey smell. Seconds later the queen was also swimming in foam.

The ants were shocked. They had never witnessed such a sight before — a frog swimming in chocolate froth — and never had their queen been so badly treated.

Lewis screwed his eyes closed and waited for the worst to happen.

A minute passed. There was utter silence. Then the queen's mouth opened and she ... hiccuped.

Lewis opened one eye. By now the froth was staining the queen's egg sac. Again she hiccuped, then rolled in the foam.

"We've killed her!" Alfonse cried. "Now we're really in trouble."

But she wasn't dead — the opposite, in fact. Her legs were kicking playfully, her antennae slapped the stone, and she was half delirious with laughter, to the point she couldn't sit on the throne. And her kicks and thrashing must have jiggled something loose. To the ants' amazement and intense delight, spheres like Ping Pong balls started spilling from her egg sac. When one such ball rolled up against Thwashkaflr, the grim adviser started laughing, as well. That set the entire colony off.

"They're laughing!" Lewis shouted. "Gibiwink made them laugh!"

"Hurray, Gibiwink!" everyone cried.

"Again my recipe turned out wrong," he groaned.

The ants kept laughing for the next few minutes, even as eggs continued to spill from the queen. It was only minutes later that the adviser called for silence.

"My friends," Thwashkaflr panted, "congratulations! Our queen — may she flourish forever — is cured and producing eggs again. True to our word, we will conduct you to the surface. In addition, we would like to thank you with a gift. Inform us of your heart's desire — diamonds, gold, we possess such treasures in abundance — and we will procure these riches instantly."

As Alfonse pictured himself with a roomful of comics, and Adelaide imagined a grand piano in their living room, and the others dreamed of other comforts, Lewis spoke on their behalf.

"Could we have a piece of the blue stone?" he gibbered.

No sooner had he spoken than the queen ripped a chunk of the stone from her seat. "I would give you the entire throne," she signalled, "if you and your friends could carry it home. You have saved our colony, and for that we are grateful."

The cavern of ants applauded again by tapping their feet against the soil. At the same time Lewis's friends started clapping, as well, understanding he had chosen wisely. They were one step closer to opening Grumpel's lock.

After expressing a few more words of gratitude, the queen ordered fifteen ants to lead their guests to the surface. Alfonse muttered that this was all a little rushed and the least they could do was throw their rescuers a party. Ants were industrious creatures, however, and with things back to normal, they wanted to return to work.

As Lewis entered a tunnel and left the cavern behind, the blue stone safely stashed in his belt, he heard the queen gibbering in the distance. Now that she had mastered the trick of laughing, she wanted to practise it as much as she could.

CHAPTER 12

The ants took them to the surface by the quickest route available. They walked through tunnels for more than an hour until they spied a crack of light in the distance — natural light and not the stone's blue glow. The friends hurried forward and, five minutes later, emerged into the fresh spring air. Everyone was happy to be outside, away from the shadows and the earth's dank smells. Their mission accomplished, the ants gibbered goodbye and hastened back to their companions below.

"Where are we?" Todrus asked, surveying the land.

"Not where we want to be," Gibiwink answered.

The group looked around. A wall of shrubbery boxed them in. It was thirty feet high, thick with roots, thorns and tubers, and seemed to extend a very great distance. And because this greenery was so densely packed, squeezing through its undergrowth was out of the question. Luckily, a path threaded the bracken, only it didn't seem to lead in any one direction.

"Where to?" Adelaide asked.

"The swamp lies that way," the Stranger said, gesturing right, "but we'll have to escape this vegetation first."

"That shouldn't be hard," Lewis said. "If we follow this path, it will lead us out eventually. And once we're in the open, we can take things from there."

The others agreed. With Todrus walking in front of them, so his broad shoulders would widen the path, they wandered off.

It wasn't easy. The path was pinched and narrow in places and full of turns and abrupt dead ends. Short of marking their course at every step, it was impossible to tell which way they were headed. And the ground was littered with roots and hollows that tripped them up at every turn, while an abundance of thorns tore at them relentlessly. Their Heliform patches were soon ripped to pieces. The growth, too, was so heavy in places that the sky's grey light could barely shine through.

"Look at that!" Gibiwink cried, spying something peculiar a few feet off the path. A thousand roots had swarmed together and overwhelmed some object at their centre.

"It's as if those shrubs were on the attack," Todrus mused. "Of course, that's impossible …"

"It's creepy," Adelaide panted. "I'll be glad when we've put this obstacle behind us."

"The Bombardier wanders in a maze," Alfonse remarked. "He's trapped in it for days and learns — ow!"

Adelaide had smacked him from behind.

They slogged on for another two hours. The path was endless. In fact, it seemed to narrow with each passing step. Everyone was sweating, and their knees were scraped raw. The dull grey sky was hopelessly distant. It was then, when their spirits couldn't sink any lower, that they spied a second tangle of roots, only this time it was set upon the path itself.

A flipper, much like Gibiwink's, projected from its middle. It was knotted with tendrils, but they recognized it still.

"How awful!" Gibiwink cried. "What happened to this frog?"

Todrus gulped. "Who knows? Let's bury him at least." That said, he grasped the flipper and tried to yank the body free. It was useless. Even when Gibiwink helped him, it was like trying to uproot a full-grown tree from the soil.

Everyone felt anxious. They had been walking forever, they were making no progress, and now this corpse was blocking their path. The one encouraging point, Lewis observed, was that a modest clearing stood a few yards off. Realizing his friends could do with a rest, he suggested they fix themselves a snack in this spot. Everyone thought that was a great idea.

They hurried to the clearing, sprayed some shrubs with their transformers, and sat down to a meal of goop. They tried not to think about the corpse nearby.

"This transformer's amazing," Gibiwink raved, savouring the food. "I wonder why Grumpel never sold it in stores. I mean, think how people's lives would improve."

"'Oo wou'n't nee' a frid'e o' stov'," Alfonse said with his mouth half full.

"And no one would go hungry," Adelaide added. "Too bad he didn't share this discovery with the world."

"He couldn't afford to," Todrus observed.

"Why's that?" Lewis asked, intrigued by this statement.

"These aren't regular transformations," the frog replied. "And the chemicals that trigger them must be very rare. For years Grumpel has been selling his inventions as if these chemicals would last forever, whereas now I suspect his supplies are running low. He's a like a fancy tailor who's used up all his silk."

"I see ..." Lewis said, his head exploding with questions. If Grumpel was running short of supplies, was that why all his factories had closed except the one in New York City? And if his chemicals were as rare as Todrus said, where had Grumpel found them to begin with? Were they somehow connected to the lock in Yellow Swamp? But why would he hide them in northern Alberta?

"Oh, my gosh!" Adelaide cried, pointing at her feet.

While she had been eating, a root had grabbed her calf. As it pinned her leg, several more sprouted up. And roots were entangling the others, as well.

"Get up everyone!" Todrus yelled. "We're under attack!"

The group obeyed, or tried to at least. Gibiwink and the Stranger tore themselves loose, but the children had a tougher time. Lewis shoved his legs sideways, cut the roots' pressure, and managed to twist himself free. But Adelaide needed help from the Stranger, while Alfonse was almost hopelessly trapped. His legs had been lassoed by a massive tuber, and if the frogs hadn't rescued him, he would have been finished. Once he was free, the tuber lunged again until Gibiwink knocked it cold with his flipper.

"Now we know what happened to that frog," Todrus gasped.

"What do you mean?" Lewis asked as the group dodged a crowd of flailing tendrils.

"These shrubs are part of one huge plant maze. The creatures inside it are forced to wander, eventually tire, and lie down to rest. At that stage —"

"The roots grab them and digest their flesh," Lewis finished.

Adelaide shuddered. "That's horrible!"

"And at the same time brilliant," Todrus proclaimed. "This strategy allows the plant to hunt down moving creatures."

"So how do we escape?" Gibiwink asked.

"When The Bombardier's inside that maze," Alfonse said, "he starts a fire and burns it to cinders. That's what we should do. In fact ..." He opened his manual and pointed to an entry. It was a recipe for a fire grenade — two drops of methylalienacrystallin, a pinch of alienahomygene, and a milligram tablet of carboalienaphophoril. After thirty seconds, the mixture would explode.

"I guess that's a good idea," Lewis said reluctantly. He was anxious to escape, but explosives made him nervous.

"It's a great idea," Alfonse insisted. Without further ado, he rummaged in his belt as the frogs assembled a "mixing base." They had to wrestle several roots as they gathered a few loose shrubs together.

"Hurry!" Todrus yelled. "This plant's growing bolder!"

"Wait a second!" Adelaide cried, examining her booklet. "It says this grenade will create a cloud of pheromones."

"What's a pheromone?" Gibiwink asked, whacking a tuber.

"It's a chemical," Todrus explained, "that animals produce —"

"Never mind!" Alfonse shouted. "We've got to escape!"

"But it warns," Adelaide continued, "that these pheromones might attract certain insects."

"Make the grenade!" Gibiwink roared, banging two large roots together.

"Get ready!" Alfonse called as he prepared the mixture. When he added the alienahomygene, the shrubs started smoking like a giant cigar.

"One, two, three …" he counted.

"Uggh! That smells terrible!" Adelaide gasped, dodging a creeper that lashed at her heels.

"Hurry!" Todrus urged Alfonse as a python-size root reared up from the soil.

"Eleven, twelve, thirteen …"

"Watch out!" the Stranger warned, saving Lewis from a tuber.

"Thanks," Lewis said, looking into its eye. For an instant he spotted something vaguely familiar. Before he could puzzle this out, a faint buzzing intruded.

"Twenty-one, twenty-two, twenty-three …"

"What's that?" Adelaide asked, cocking an ear.

"Who cares? Throw the grenade!" Todrus yelled. A sprawling three-pronged sprout was out to get him.

"Twenty-eight, twenty-nine, thirty!" Alfonse cried, pitching the grenade at the tangle straight in front of him. It spiralled into the thick of the scrub, belching smoke that made everyone cough. Then it exploded with a brilliant flash, and a wave of heat rolled outward. It was lucky their clothes had been fireproofed — and the Stranger's bark-like skin was tough — since the ensuing flames would have cooked them to a turn.

Some seconds passed before they opened their eyes. One after another they raised a cheer: the blast had blown a gaping hole in the plant, and a plain was visible beyond the scorched vegetation.

"We've done it!" Alfonse whooped. "The plant's been busted open!"

"Let's get out of here!" Todrus cried, motioning to a charred root that was starting to jiggle.

Following his lead, the travellers hurtled past the hole and didn't stop running until they had covered a mile, and even then they stared at the ground in suspicion. Alfonse flinched at one point — a severed root was on his back — but bit by bit they began to relax.

They fell to the ground, panting. After their trek underground and their walk through the maze, they were in desperate need of a rest. They were about to close their eyes, in fact, when again a distant buzzing reached Adelaide's ears.

"What's that sound?" she asked. "I heard it when the grenade was smoking."

"It doesn't matter," Alfonse muttered. "Let's get some rest."

"It's off-key," she insisted, "and it's getting closer"

Alfonse glowered. "Never mind! Everyone's tired."

Even as he spoke, a bulbous shape zipped by. It moved so quickly that no one caught a good look. Gibiwink, however, claimed he had spotted its eyes and said they were huge and split into sections, as if they were covered with window screening.

"Those sound like the eyes on a fly," Todrus murmured.

"The pheromones must have attracted it," Adelaide added.

The group exchanged looks of disgust — even the frogs, who had eaten plenty of flies in their time.

"It's coming back," Adelaide warned. "Can you hear its off-key buzzing?"

"Who cares?" Alfonse sneered. "All I know is that fly's bugging me. If it comes any closer, it's going to regret it!"

No sooner had he spoken than the insect returned. And instead of zinging by, it alighted on a nearby patch of earth and filled the air with the smell of rotting garbage. Lewis shivered slightly. It was three feet long and a foot and a half wide. Its surface bristled with a million hairs, each as black and shiny as oil, while its wings twitched with inhuman speed, striking up a string of notes, all of them off-key. Its eyes reflected the group a hundred times over.

The worst part was the creature's clippers. They were five inches long and looked a lot like scissors.

"That's no ordinary fly," Gibiwink whispered. "That's —"

"A black fly!" Adelaide broke in. "Only a thousand times bigger!"

Todrus whistled. "And its clippers mean business."

"It's still just a fly," Alfonse scoffed. "I'll teach it not to pester us!" He lifted a clod of earth. Before the group could stop him, he hit the fly head-on. With bits of soil clinging to its hairs, the fly took wing, wobbling slightly. Alfonse laughed. "Did you see that? It won't be back in a hurry!"

"That was stupid," Adelaide said. "It didn't look happy."

"When my family camped here two summers ago," Lewis said, "it was near the end of the black fly season. For the first couple of days they almost drove us crazy."

"Listen!" Todrus cried, motioning them to silence. As the group fell quiet, they heard an off-key whine, one that filled the sky from top to bottom, as if an orchestra were playing but its instruments weren't tuned. At the same time a black cloud was taking shape in the distance and making its way toward the group. Within seconds it covered the sky above them.

"I … I don't like this!" Adelaide stammered.

As the cloud hovered a hundred feet away, a single fly descended and alighted on a stone. By the earth in its hairs, they knew it was the fly from before. The group waved and signalled their apologies, but it sped off with a twist of its wings, as if to say the shoe was on the other foot. The buzzing became a thousand times louder.

"What a smell!" Gibiwink yelled, covering his nose.

"Never mind that!" Todrus screamed, thrusting Alfonse and Adelaide behind him. He would have sheltered Lewis, too, but the Stranger had grabbed him and had its tentacles upraised. "They're about to attack! Get ready to fight!"

On its first swoop the swarm knocked the friends off their feet. In addition to the smell and clacking clippers, there was the awful racket to deal with.

Even on his back, Todrus lashed out at the flies, forcing five to veer off course and smash into their neighbours, until thirty of them wound up crashing to earth. Gibiwink clobbered two, as well, and the Stranger bagged another.

"They mean to kill us!" Todrus hollered as the swarm backed off for a moment. "Find some concoction that will chase them away!"

"There's no recipe for bug spray!" Lewis cried. "I searched for it earlier!"

The flies swooped again. Although they didn't quite hit anyone, they drove the group crazy with their off-key buzzing. The frogs and Stranger punched away, Adelaide and Alfonse tossed clods of earth, and Lewis continued to flip madly through his book's index.

"There's nothing here!" he shouted.

The third pass was worse. The frogs scored a couple of strikes but got wounded in turn. Gibiwink took a bite on the shoulder, and Todrus's skull was repeatedly knocked. The Stranger, too, didn't get off easy — two of its tentacles were nicked all over. One fly threatened Adelaide, but Alfonse stepped in. Leaping onto the insect's back, he poked its eyes and hammered it all over. Abandoning Adelaide, it soared into the swarm ... with Alfonse clutching it still.

"Jump!" Adelaide called to him.

"I'm too high!" he cried faintly, "and my Heliform patch is gone!"

"Alfonse!" Adelaide screamed again in a high, near-deafening tone.

Alfonse didn't answer. He was lost in the swarm.

But it was odd. The flies were at a momentary standstill. They had been about to strike again but were suddenly dazed and twitching all over ... until the last of Adelaide's shrieks died off. Seconds later their confidence returned, and they pressed in for the kill, more aggressively than ever.

A thought struck Lewis. "Adelaide! Start singing!"

"What?"

"Start singing! They can't stand perfect notes! That's what rattled them when you screamed just now! Start singing quickly. Any song will do!"

A hundred flies were hounding Todrus. Gibiwink was on his back, beating back a dozen clippers. The Stranger, too, was fading fast. With a look of fear, Adelaide sang out.

It was a song by Johann Sebastian Bach — her favourite composer. Although the words were in German and the situation was desperate, Lewis thought it was beautiful. More to the point, it was very effective. As soon as the flies caught wind of the notes, their buzzing grew faint and they abandoned the group. Seeing this, Adelaide straightened herself. She repeated the song in a clear, flawless voice that cut through the swarm and its awful aroma, penetrating straight to the heavens.

The group eyed Adelaide with newfound respect — they hadn't known she could sing with such power — but the flies themselves were only disgusted. Their one thought was to escape the awful noise. Moving as one, they raced toward the horizon, vanishing as quickly as they had appeared.

But the ordeal wasn't over. As soon as the flies' last

echo had died, the group moved forward across the grassy plain. Lewis and Adelaide were noticeably distressed.

"Alfonse!" they called.

The plain was enormous, so the group split up. Long minutes passed as they scoured the terrain, ignoring the dead flies littering the landscape. The air kept ringing with shouts of "Alfonse!" and Lewis grew frantic as his friend failed to answer. Had the flies taken him prisoner? Would they hurt him in revenge for the defeat they had suffered?

"Over here!" Adelaide called from a hundred yards off. "Over here!" she repeated in a muted voice.

Charging to her side, Lewis saw that her face was frozen over. She was standing over something … no, that object was Alfonse, only his body seemed so tiny and was strangely motionless. And the earth surrounding him was soaked with blood.

Blood? No! That couldn't be! In their manuals they would find —

"We're too late!" Adelaide wailed. "My brother's dead!"

CHAPTER 13

ewis was paralyzed. Adelaide's words had turned his legs to stone. In a trance he watched as Todrus took Alfonse's pulse, shook his head sadly, and confirmed the heart had stopped beating. It wasn't possible. How could this have happened to Alfonse? For sure he was pretending and would jump up soon to blurt out something about The Bombardier.

But he didn't move a muscle. His face was pale and empty.

"He can't be dead!" Adelaide bawled. "I always insulted him because of his size, yet he died protecting me! I'm so ashamed!"

Lewis wanted to say he was sorry, but he couldn't blink or bend his fingers. The Stranger stared at the soil, and Gibiwink kept saying it was all his fault, that he should have done a better job of protecting Alfonse. Todrus leaned over the body and examined it closely. A flash of silver appeared in his flipper.

"What now?" the Stranger murmured. "We can't leave him like this."

"What do you mean?" Interrupting her sobs, Adelaide glared at the creature.

"We have to keep moving. Those flies might return.

That means we either carry Alfonse, or ... well ... I'm sorry ... we bury him here."

"Bury him?" Adelaide shrieked. "You want to bury him in this awful region? Here in Alberta, a million miles from home? Never! I won't hear of it!"

She dissolved into tears. Everyone felt terrible and didn't know what to do. That was when Todrus opened his palm and disclosed a silver vial inside. It bore a tiny cap, which he struggled to open with his oversize flippers.

"I recognize that vial," Lewis croaked. "That's the one Elizabeth Grumpel was wearing. She lost it on the chopper when we knocked into each other."

Todrus chuckled. "Actually, I stole it from her."

"Stole it?" Lewis said. "Why?"

At that moment the cap popped open, and a pill rolled out. Todrus caught it just in time.

Despite their grief, the group stared at the pill. It glimmered in an unearthly fashion and wobbled slightly as if it were alive.

"Back in Grumpel's office," Todrus said, steadying his flipper so the pill wouldn't slip, "Elizabeth mentioned an *elixir vitae*, and Grumpel quickly shut her up."

"Who cares? My brother's dead. What difference —"

"He's dead, exactly" Todrus agreed. "So it doesn't matter if I experiment, does it?"

He opened Alfonse's mouth, placed the pill inside, and closed the jaw quickly as if worried the substance might fly away. Everyone watched with bated breath.

A minute passed and nothing happened.

"I don't understand," Adelaide said. She was thinking how her brother's death would come as such a blow to her parents. "What are you expecting this pill to do?"

"For centuries chemists have searched for a mixture that would bring a dead man back to life. They called this substance the *elixir vitae* — the recipe of life. While no one ever found this elixir, I suspect this pill is what they were seeking."

"That's ridiculous!" Adelaide cried. "Once someone's dead, he's gone forever! You shouldn't be talking such hocus-pocus!"

She was about to turn away when Lewis grabbed her and pointed at her brother's eyes. Was something happening, or was it a trick of the light? Yes, there, the pupils were changing. Whereas they had been blank the moment before, their sparkle of old was quickly returning. His body, too, was suffused with a glow — the same radiance coming from the weird-looking pill — and the pallor was being drained from his cheeks like ice cream melting beneath a summer sun.

"What on earth?" Adelaide murmured. In his excitement Gibiwink had looped his tongue around her neck.

"His heart's beating!" Todrus whispered, measuring Alfonse's pulse.

"And the blood on the ground is disappearing!" Lewis cried, pointing to the stain that was rapidly fading as if Alfonse were absorbing the blood like a sponge. By now his chest was heaving visibly, his lips were twitching, and his skin was pink.

"But has his brain been affected?" Adelaide asked.

"Justice and thunder," Alfonse moaned, a favourite saying of The Bombardier.

"He's the same!" Lewis yelled with relief.

Adelaide laughed. "I never thought I'd be so happy to hear those words!"

As the group looked on, Alfonse stood up, glanced at his surroundings, and collected his thoughts. Lewis worried again that Alfonse's brain wasn't right, but when his friend delivered him The Bombardier signal — three winks and a wriggle of the thumbs — he was sure Alfonse was back to normal.

Or was he?

"What's that smell?" Alfonse asked, sniffing the air.

"What smell?" everyone wondered.

"It smells like candy, no, like caramel," Alfonse said. "And keep it down, will you? There's no need to shout."

"Caramel?" The frogs were sniffing, as well. "That's strange. We can't smell anything."

Alfonse waved to their left. "It's coming from over there. Past that bush with the bird's nest and the patch of grey moss."

The group followed his finger. All they saw was an unfolding meadow with clumps of grass and meandering patches of mist.

"It's before that forest and the mountain that's covered in fog," Alfonse cried, like an adult explaining simple facts to a child.

Forest? Mountain? They shrugged at one another.

"This is ridiculous!" Alfonse spat. "Just follow me!"

Before they could stop him, he started off. Because his legs were so much shorter than average, Alfonse had never been much of a runner. When he set off after the caramel smell, however, there was no keeping up. He ran like a cheetah and was gone in a flash. His friends were dumbfounded.

"It's the pill!" Todrus said as they rushed off in pursuit. "Besides bringing him back, it's enhanced his senses."

"That ... sounds ... about ... right," Lewis gasped.

"Let's ... find ... him," Adelaide panted. "Don't ... want ... him ... dying ... again!"

For fifteen minutes they ran full throttle. As he tried not to trip in the odd, hidden hollow, Lewis thought about his friend's rescue from death. Of course, he was delighted. At the same time, though, he found Alfonse's recovery disturbing. There was something about these chemicals that made him suspicious. Life was never supposed to be this easy. It wasn't right that food appeared from nowhere, requiring no time to be gathered and cooked. And languages weren't supposed to come in a pill. As for death itself, well, as frightening as it seemed, and as glad as he was that Alfonse was alive, surely it was a force that was bigger than humans. In other words, these chemicals were a mockery of nature —

"There!" Adelaide cried, interrupting his thoughts. "Alfonse ... right ... really ... is ... bird's ... nest!"

Sure enough, beside a long patch of moss, a gorse bush sheltered a nest in its middle.

"We're in luck," Todrus added. "He's left prints in the moss and we can follow his trail."

"Must ... run ... faster," Adelaide urged them. "Can't ... lose ... him ... again!"

They ran full tilt for another five minutes, crashing through the grass and dodging the odd thicket. A spiral of mist absorbed them briefly, then the view in front of them was suddenly clear.

Alfonse was standing a hundred yards off. He was poised on an incline at the start of a clearing and was gazing ahead with his hands on his hips.

"Alfonse!" the frogs and the Stranger cried. Lewis and Adelaide couldn't spare any breath.

"Didn't I tell you not to shout?" Alfonse snapped.

At the foot of the incline they dropped to the ground, puffing hard and trembling all over. Alfonse for his part was completely relaxed and looked as if he could keep on running forever. It was eerie, this newfound power of his.

"I told you I smelled caramel," he observed. "It's coming from those flowers."

Lewis flinched. He had been running so hard that he hadn't noticed the smell. Alfonse was right. It was just like caramel. But what flowers was he pointing to?

"Let's see," Lewis said wearily, joining his friend on the incline. With a groan the others clawed up behind him. The sight that greeted them was worth the effort.

They were standing on a shelf of earth that overlooked a field. The tract ran on for perhaps a mile and was festooned with flowers by the thousands and thousands. The flowers were laden with shocking pink petals, and a smell of caramel hung over the soil.

Beyond the flowers was the start of a forest, whose trees had obviously been through a fire. And beyond their ruined trunks — a heartbreaking sight — a rugged mountain loomed over the land, shrouded in mist and barely visible. Alfonse was studying its crest with interest.

"The swamp's past that mountain," the Stranger said.

Adelaide laughed. "Forget the mountain. How often do you see daffodils like these?"

"Daffodils!" Lewis cried.

"They're pink and smell like caramel," Todrus said, grasping Lewis's train of thought. "In fact —"

"They're the flowers in the poem!" everyone yelled.

"So what are we waiting for?" Alfonse demanded. Without hesitating he jumped into the thick of the flowers. Not wanting to lose sight of him, the others followed.

The flowers were even prettier than they had seemed from afar. Each was maybe three feet wide and heavy with petals that were smooth and fleshy. As he passed these fleecy masses — they reminded him of mattresses — Lewis was tempted to lie down and sleep.

Then his foot caught on something. It was long and hard and rough to the touch. He sprang back in alarm. Sprawled at his feet, half buried in flowers, was a salamander that was easily the size of a car. Its long, lean body projected prodigious strength, its feet were armed with deadly claws, and its massive tail could have been used as a bludgeon.

Fortunately, the creature hadn't spotted him yet. It was lying still and paying no notice. Fixing his eyes on the beast, Lewis backed away ... only to knock into a giant snake!

The salamander was tiny compared to this new, lurking danger. The coils — a loathsome green and unthinkably destructive — were maybe eight feet wide and twisted in and out of the flowers. The serpent's head was no less frightening. It stood a couple of yards from Lewis and was as big as a fridge and covered with scales.

While the eyes were closed, the mouth was open and revealed fangs as long as an elephant's tusks.

As Lewis eyed this reptile, its eyes flickered open. Yellow, hard, and inhuman they were, bigger than searchlights and projecting ... death. At the same time its tongue came lunging forward, bloody pink and clustered with veins. Its tip rubbed his ankles and ... He almost screamed. Before the sounds could escape, however, the tongue curled past him, latched onto a flower, plucked several petals, and returned to its mouth. The snake's eyes closed, and it went back to sleep.

As Lewis searched for his friends — they were standing nearby — he saw that the field was crowded with creatures — frogs, salamanders, turtles, and snakes. All of them were giant-size and all were sleeping.

"I don't like this," Alfonse said, tiptoeing next to Lewis.

"I don't, either. I'm just glad that snake's a vegetarian."

"Let's not take any chances," Adelaide warned. "Let's pluck a petal and get out of here before these creatures catch wind of our presence."

"They're not interested in us," the Stranger said. It was standing near the snake and had an ear against its coils.

"How do you know?" Todrus asked, studying a frog that was twice his size and lying in the flowers with a dreamy expression.

"This snake is talking in its sleep," the Stranger answered. "That translation brew is affecting me still and I can understand it."

"What's it saying?" everyone asked at once.

"It keeps repeating 'Flowers, forget, sleep, forget' over and over. The other beasts are saying the same."

"How did that poem go?" Lewis asked.

"'Unless joined with forgetful daffodil / with petals pink and scent of caramel …'" the Stranger recited.

The group put two and two together. The flower contained a chemical that caused a creature's memories to fade. These beasts weren't asleep but in a state of oblivion and had forgotten everything about their past. The snake hadn't bothered with Lewis because, thanks to the petals, it didn't know about its fangs.

"I imagine," the Stranger said with a frown, "that these creatures can probably think like us. They must have found this change confusing — if you're not used to it, a powerful brain can be dreadful — and when they learned these flowers would let them forget, well, you can see the results for yourselves."

Everyone nodded, their expressions pale. Now that they understood the daffodil's effects, that its chemicals would rob them of their memories if eaten, they found it more frightening than the reptiles around them. The thought of lying there for months on end unable to remember themselves or their friends, with no clue whatsoever who they were … It was the worst possible fate they could think of.

"I've stored a petal in my pouch," Lewis said.

"Then let's go," Adelaide recommended.

That said she ran toward the forest in the distance, her eyes searching for any creature in her path. The others bounded after her, Lewis last of all.

For the first hundred yards he was as scared as the

others. As he watched them dodge among the flowers, however, and flinch every time the petals grazed their skin, he began to reconsider his fears.

Forgetfulness. Yes. On the one hand, it seemed awful — was there anything worse than forgetting all your memories? On the other hand, he was tired of the constant ache. He was tired of feeling sorrow when he saw his mother's picture or worked with his locks or watched children with their parents. It was always there, always. And his father, too, was on the verge of disappearing ...

The others were well ahead of him. They were anxious to reach the end of the field and hadn't yet noticed that he had fallen behind. In fact, he was gazing at the sleeping creatures and envying them their tranquil state. The flowers, too, grabbed his eye, with their luxuriant petals that promised freedom from the hardship and sadness of the world. His hand reached out and stroked one petal. With the slightest tug he freed it from its moorings. *To sleep, to forget, to escape the pain.* The petal was more than halfway to his mouth ...

And yet ...

His memories of his mother's smile, her songs and laughter, their lessons together — weren't these keeping her alive in some sense? As soon as *he* forgot her loving kindness and allowed her actions to slip away, wouldn't *he* be killing her all over again? His ache, as hard as it was at times, was a tribute to his mother, a recognition of her presence. It was, in fact, his most precious possession.

A wave of shame poured over him. Dropping the petal, he turned toward his friends who had reached the field's limits by now and were urging him forward. He bounded toward them. Skirting one creature after the next, he pushed himself as hard as he could to escape this paradise that contained death at its centre.

CHAPTER

14

Lewis was trying to keep his eyes open. For the past half-hour, over a meal of goop, the group had been discussing their best course of action. Should they camp where they were on the verge of the forest and scour the region for the last ingredient? Or should they search for it en route to Yellow Swamp, on the grounds they would be killing two birds with one stone? They were exhausted and couldn't make up their minds.

"It's like a needle in a haystack," Adelaide grumbled for the third time in the past ten minutes.

"Then let's head for the swamp *now*," Todrus yawned. "At least we'll make some progress that way."

"But we've got to find the weed," she protested. "And that might mean retracing our steps."

"Unless the weed's near the swamp," Gibiwink argued. And so the discussion dragged on and on.

There might have been a quarrel had Alfonse not spoken up. He had been strangely quiet for the whole exchange and was seated several feet away from the group. "I know where we can find that weed."

Everyone started, and Lewis's eyes jumped open.

As the group pressed Alfonse to explain himself, he gestured to the mountain that overshadowed the forest. "When we were on that hill overlooking the flowers, I managed to get a close look at the mountain and saw a giant oak growing on its crest. In its highest branches there's a yellow-tipped weed, exactly like the one described in the poem."

"Are you sure?" Todrus asked. "Your eyes would have to be sharp."

"I'm sure," Alfonse snapped. "You'll find the weed in that tree."

"You should have said so earlier!" Adelaide muttered. "We've been discussing our plans for over an hour."

Alfonse shrugged. "I was distracted. My powers are gone." That said, he moved away from the group and propped himself at the foot of an alder.

Feeling bad for Alfonse, Lewis strolled over. "Move over." He sat next to his friend. "I'm sorry about your powers."

Alfonse yawned. "You shouldn't be. I'm happy they're gone."

"You are? You don't mind?"

"I know this sounds strange, but those powers were creepy. When I was running fast and could see things at a distance, it felt like a stranger was working inside me. Besides, I should be dead right now."

"What's it like?" Lewis whispered. "Being dead, I mean."

"It felt … it was like …" Alfonse sought the right words. "I was far away, very far away, beyond reach of everything, both good and evil. It's nice to be back, that's all I can say, and you won't ever hear me complaining again."

Lewis stood and tapped his friend's shoulder. He was about to suggest the group start moving when he noticed that the others had fallen asleep. Lewis shook the frogs vigorously but couldn't get them to stir. Glancing back, he saw that Alfonse had dropped off, too.

As Lewis stood there wondering what he should do, exhaustion hit him with the force of a hammer, almost knocking him off his feet. Maybe a nap would do him good, he thought. After all, as his father often argued, rest was the formula for all success.

His father. Lewis frowned. Again he saw his dad in that sunken chamber, frozen, weakened, with those guards poised above him. He had looked so helpless, so utterly defeated.

"I can't afford to sleep," Lewis gasped, reaching for his manual. "He'll die if we don't reach him soon."

Focusing hard to stay awake, Lewis searched the book for a possible solution. He wound up making two discoveries. The first involved the chemicals themselves — it turned out they were all related to one another. Even as he kicked himself for having missed this connection, he came across a most promising entry: "Sleep compression," the index read.

Following the directions, he pulled out vials of hydralienic microsulfate, alienodextrose, and chlorolacticalienamalinamine. He was barely able to keep his eyes open, but he managed to pour these ingredients onto a handful of dirt and grimaced when a slimy violet gel took shape. Steeling himself, he swallowed part of it. *Yuck!*

Lewis waited. Was it working? He didn't feel any

different. Sniffing with impatience, he glanced up at the sky. A chip from a tree was falling toward him, bullet-shaped and black as coal. He tried to catch it, but a wave of grey bowled him over.

He was falling, falling, falling. A corridor appeared. It was lined with a trophy case and newspaper clippings, each with a story about Ernst K. Grumpel. One headline read METEORITE IN MASON SPRINGS! while a second trumpeted PHARMACIST SCORES TRIUMPH! A moment later he was at the door to a pool. The chain on its handles opened without warning, and three hulking figures emerged. One pointed a rifle at him. He cried, "Don't shoot!" But the figure only laughed and pulled the trigger.

Lewis awoke with a start. Despite this jarring nightmare, he had slept like the dead and had never felt quite so rested before. He yawned, stretched, and thought about his dream. Then a bolt of panic caused him to tremble. How long had he been down? Four hours? Six? Eight? Ten? Twelve? His father was clinging to life by a thread and he had dared —

A wood chip hit him. It was bullet-shaped and black as coal. Lewis frowned, then laughed. It was the chip he had spied before the brew had kicked in and, as incredible as it seemed, he had been asleep for five seconds!

"Alfonse!" he cried, scooping up some gel. "Try this mixture! It'll leave you feeling rested."

Because his friend didn't respond, Lewis fed him the substance. He repeated this process with the rest of the gang, opening their jaws and placing the mix inside. By the time he had finished, the gel was taking effect.

"Boy, did I sleep!" Alfonse declared.

"Me, too!" the rest of the group sang out. Weak and exhausted only minutes before, they were all on their feet and itching to move forward.

"All right," Lewis said, "we know where to go to find the weed. Let's head for the mountain, track the weed down, and end this mission once and for all!"

His friends thought this was an excellent idea. With a heartening shout they set off together, leaving the open field behind and plunging into the thick of the forest. As they marched, they swapped jokes and encouraged one another, confident their goal was finally within reach.

A minute later their spirits sank once more.

The woods had been blasted through and through. Once a collection of birch, pine, and alder, it was now black and charred and maimed all over. Not a single speck of green was visible, and the branches were scarred, gnarled, and twisted, as if they were doubled over in pain. The bark, too, was hideous, like the skin on someone who had been burned all over. The worst part was the silence: there were no bird songs, no cricket calls, no rustling leaves. And at every step they sank up to their ankles in ash.

What a pity, Lewis thought. Normally, he was fond of nature — he loved the Canadian wilds, for example — but this forest's desolation made him sick at heart. To distract himself and his friends from the carnage, he described his dream about the trophy case and clippings.

"You were back in school," Alfonse suggested.

"Yes. The clippings were about that meteorite and how Grumpel became a sensation soon after —"

"Like in real life," Adelaide interrupted, half stumbling in the ash.

"That's my point. The dream was telling me something."

"Like what?" Todrus asked.

Lewis replied that he didn't know. On the other hand, he had a discovery to share — how the chemicals in their belts had something in common. Before he could explain further, the forest erupted.

There was no wind present, yet the branches swayed and creaked on high, never mind all of them were horrifically battered. The friends glanced up. The trees were rubbing their boughs together, not casually as happened when a breeze arose, but like fiddlers sawing away on their bows.

"I know this sounds crazy," Lewis shouted to make himself heard above the wild scratching, "but I'd swear these trees were talking to each other!"

"They are." Again, because of the translation brew, the Stranger was able to decipher these sounds. "They think you're murderers, as a matter of fact."

"Murderers? Us?" the group cried out.

"That's what they're saying," the Stranger insisted. "I think it has something to do with your outfits."

"That's crazy!" Alfonse argued. "These outfits aren't ours! Grumpel forced us to put them on."

"But don't you see?" Adelaide interrupted. "*His* henchmen wrecked this region, along with these trees. And I suspect —"

"They were dressed just like us," Lewis finished. "And that means these trees think we're working for Grumpel."

They hurried on in silence. The trees continued to

scratch and saw, then started spitting bark at the group. Now that the Stranger had translated the racket, everyone could sense the raw hatred. Infuriated on account of their wounds, these trees were intent on exacting revenge.

Lewis felt uneasy, if not for himself, then for his mother at least. He thought back to Elizabeth's statement about his mother. She had told him that his mother had informed Grumpel about Yellow Swamp's existence and that, if not for her, this part of Alberta would be unscathed. Although his mother had loved nature deeply and would never have been part of Grumpel's scheme — if she had known it would mean the swamp's ruin — this disaster was partially her doing. She had been so intent on building an unbreakable lock that everything else had been forgotten.

"Ow!" Todrus wailed as a piece of bark struck home. The trees were now attacking in earnest and tossing large parts of themselves at the group, in some cases branches that could crush them flat. And the scratching was loud, not to mention insulting. If they stayed there much longer, they would be killed for sure.

"Let's run for it!" Lewis yelled, pointing at the mountain ahead. A hundred yards off, in the midst of the forest, a mass of rocks rose up from the soil and stormed its way straight into the clouds.

With the trees hurling threats and jeers in their wake, not to mention a volley of missiles, they doubled their speed and dodged a tangle of roots. One branch fell straight toward Lewis and would have crushed him had the Stranger not knocked it aside. One second later and —

"Thanks," Lewis gasped.

"My pleasure," the Stranger answered, returning his gaze.

Again, for an instant, Lewis spied something familiar.

The trees were so furious that, even when the travellers reached the base of the mountain, they didn't pause to catch their breath. Instead they scrambled toward its boulders and started climbing for all they were worth.

The ascent wasn't difficult, in the technical sense, since there were plenty of ledges and cracks to clutch onto. Still, the face was frighteningly steep. By the time they had covered the first hundred yards, the easiest part of the climb, everyone was sweating and fighting for breath. It wasn't wise to look down, either. There were no lack of footholds, but the drop was … lethal.

They continued climbing for the next half-hour, unable to speak because they were puffing so hard. By now the trees were far below, yet they had conquered only part of the mountain, as if they were ants on a human being and had only reached the start of his knees. The rock was sharp and cut their skin, yet they clung to it the way a baby nuzzled its parent.

"Ooh," Gibiwink moaned, pausing to glance below. "Did I ever mention I'm hydrophobic?"

"You're scared of water?" Todrus panted.

"Is that what it means? Then I'm looking for another word … xenophobic?"

"The proper word is acrophobic — a fear of heights," Todrus lectured. "Xenophobia is the fear of strangers, anyone who's not from the same place as you."

"Speaking of things from somewhere else," Lewis gasped. "Have any of you noticed something strange about the chemicals we've been using?"

"You're kidding, right?" Alfonse asked, dropping a stone and watching it fall to the soil. "I mean, these chemicals are *only* strange."

Lewis produced a handful of vials. He then read the words printed on the labels. "*Alieno*phloxyxene, hydr*alieno*plasmic acid, tyr*aliena*hippaceronase, menin-aeide*alieno*theacide …"

"I don't get it," Alfonse said.

Lewis laughed. "It's staring you in the face. Each vial contains something with *alieno* or *aliena* in the name. Let's call it Alienus. You're a chemist, Todrus. Does that sound familiar?"

The frog frowned. "Alienus? Hmm, there's no such thing."

"You mean, there's no such thing on Earth," Lewis corrected.

"Now hang on a second. Are you suggesting …?"

Lewis nodded. "This substance is from another planet. And it arrived on the meteorite that fell on Grumpel's farm, the one reported in that newspaper clipping."

"You mean Grumpel's inventions —" Alfonse asked.

"Exactly. How else would he have become an overnight sensation? When that meteorite landed, it was carrying an element."

"Alienus," the Stranger mused.

Lewis smiled. "Which can trigger all sorts of amazing reactions. Grumpel must have found that out and quickly built an empire for himself."

The group exchanged worried frowns with one another. They didn't like this conversation. The thought that they were carrying a foreign substance like that, an element from a far-off galaxy perhaps, sent tingles up and down their spines. Was there life on other planets? Was something, somewhere, watching from … out there?

"And that's why he's been closing his factories," Lewis added. "He's running low on Alienus and can't mass-produce his inventions any longer — just as Todrus argued."

Alfonse whistled. "So that's what he's hiding in Yellow Swamp. Piles and piles of Alienus."

"There's more to it than that," Adelaide said. "I mean, he could have hidden this stuff in New York City and had it available when the first batch failed. So what's it doing in northern Alberta?"

"And why did he cause that chemical spill?" the Stranger added.

"You're right," Todrus said after a pause. "We haven't solved the entire riddle. Still, we won't find answers by lounging about. Let's collect the weed, get to the swamp, and see what this mystery's about for ourselves."

They continued the ascent. Apart from the heavy effort it required, the odd, tense moment when someone missed his footing, and the breathtaking but dizzying view of the landscape, the rest of the climb was uneventful. Eventually, Alfonse mounted a boulder, only to discover he had reached the top.

"We've done it!" he cried. "We're at the crest!"

"Thank goodness," Gibiwink sighed, his flippers scraped all over.

"Let's celebrate," Todrus wheezed. "And fix ourselves a snack."

"We'd be celebrating too soon," Adelaide objected.

Everyone followed her pointing finger, and one by one their looks of triumph faded. The mountain had so distracted them, as had their talk about Alienus, that they had forgotten why they were scaling its heights.

A gargantuan oak stood a short distant off. Its trunk rose hundreds of feet into the air, only to vanish in a bank of mist. There was no saying how tall it was. Its width, too, was just as impressive. If they joined hands, they would encircle half its trunk. No branches were visible, high or low, and the bark had the same smoothness as steel.

Lewis gulped and passed a hand through his hair. The *real* climb hadn't even started yet.

CHAPTER 15

"So how are we going to climb this thing?" Alfonse demanded for the umpteenth time. They were sitting in a circle and picking at some goop. Every so often they paused in mid-bite, craned their necks, and studied the oak. It didn't seem like a tree as much as a pillar holding the sky in place.

"The question is 'who?' not 'how?'" Todrus mused. "I, for one, am a terrible climber. There's no way I can scale a tree like that."

"I'm scared of heights," Gibiwink whined, a statement the Pangettis and the Stranger repeated.

Lewis had been flipping through his manual all the while. Now he spoke. "My dad's the one in danger. I'll climb that tree."

Ashamed, the others stopped eating. Explaining how they hadn't meant to stick him with this job, they suggested they should flip a coin or something. But Lewis had decided. He himself would go.

"But how?" Alfonse asked. "The trunk is huge, the bark is smooth, and you can't even see where the branches begin."

"This is a long shot," Lewis admitted, "but there's an entry in the manual for *metallization*. It lets you coat any surface with a layer of steel."

"How's that going to help?"

"I'll mix the brew and you'll see what I'm thinking." Lewis took three vials from his belt and combined their contents on a wide, flat stone. Then he retreated several feet as the rock changed colour.

"It smells like something burning," Alfonse commented.

"No wonder," Adelaide said, examining the mixture. "The stone's been changed to liquid metal."

She was right. Before them was a pool of grey that a breeze was rippling slightly. Lewis drew near it. His feet were bare.

"What are you doing?" the Stranger asked as Lewis stooped and spread his fingers wide. "And why did you remove your shoes and socks?"

"Lewis!" the others warned … to no avail. He dipped his fingers in the pool as far as the first joints. Grimacing as his fingertips turned to metal, he then stuck his toes into the mixture, as well.

"Have you gone crazy?" Adelaide fumed as Lewis flexed his fingers and toes to prevent the joints from hardening. A moment later he tapped them against a stone. Just as he had hoped, the tips were hard and razor-sharp.

Lewis leaped at the tree and struck it with his "claws." They sank into the bark and let him cling to its surface. His belt, however, got in the way. Jumping to the ground, he unfastened its straps — being careful not to slash himself — and handed it over to Todrus for safekeeping. It pained him to leave his supply belt behind, but the climb would be more manageable without it. Unencumbered, he "jumped" the tree a second time.

"That's clever," Todrus said as Lewis clung to the bark. "But do you think you can make it to the top and back?"

"And your Heliform patch is gone," Alfonse warned. "If you fall —"

"I have no choice," Lewis said, extracting his toes to dig them in higher, then doing the same with both his hands. He would be okay as long as his strength held out … and he stopped himself from looking down.

"Be careful!" the group advised as Lewis set off in earnest.

It was a lot like swimming. Left foot, right hand, right foot, left hand, over and over — there was nothing to it. And his progress was impressive. Within minutes he climbed more than fifty yards. At that rate he would reach the top in no time at all.

Left foot, right hand, right foot, left hand.

After two hundred yards, he crossed into the mist. It was nothing like the Pother — he could see his fingers still — but it stopped him from hearing his friends' shouts below. With luck he would stumble on a branch soon enough.

Left foot, right hand, right foot, left hand.

He was panting like an engine, and sweat was stinging his eyes. As much as he wanted to wipe his face, he couldn't risk taking a hand off the bark. His joints were sore and his muscles burned. When would those low branches appear?

Left foot, right hand, right foot, left hand.

How high had he climbed? How much higher could he go before his strength petered out — three hundred yards, if even that? And was that enough to get him to the branches, assuming there *were* branches? And if he *did* reach the branches, how much farther was the top? And would he find the weed as Alfonse had predicted?

That was odd. His left grip was unsteady and his pinky was sore.

Left foot, right hand, right foot, left hand.

The pain was getting worse. Ignoring the risk, he paused and peered at his hand. His blood ran cold. The coating on his pinky had failed! He had known the brew wouldn't last forever but had thought it would be good for several hours at least. This was bad. This was very bad.

He climbed more frantically. *Left foot, right hand, right foot, left hand, left foot, right hand, right foot, left hand.*

Ow! His left index finger was bare, his right pinky, too, and various toes were starting to go. His hold was growing more and more precarious.

Left foot, right hand, right foot, left hand, left foot, right foot, right hand.

No! A mere two fingers on his right hand were metallic. The bark of the tree, obscured by the mist, smiled at him mockingly, as if it liked the idea of him falling to earth in payment for the wounds his metal claws were inflicting.

Left foot, right hand, right foot, left hand.

Most of his fingers and toes were useless. His muscles were shaking and his strength was almost gone. If only his Heliform patch were intact!

Left foot, right hand, right foot, left hand.

What remained? His right thumb, left index finger, and maybe three toes. In another thirty seconds, if not sooner, he would plunge through the air with nothing to catch him. He pictured his father, weak and frozen over. Once Lewis crashed to earth, his companions would leave — probably to meet up with some horrible end — and Grumpel would starve his father to death. So it had all been in vain. The quest was a failure.

Left foot, right hand, right foot, left hand, left foot, right hand.

Lewis's grip was weakening. Numbly, he wondered what death was like. According to Alfonse, it wasn't that painful. How had his friend described it — that he had felt far away. Lewis had asked his mother about death, years before, when he was four or five. She had said it was a mystery but that the best parts of people lingered on because nature would never let love go to waste. In a matter of seconds he would find out for himself.

Left foot, right hand, right foot, left hand, left foot, right hand.

Ow! What the heck?

He had struck his head.

"What's going on?" he cried, only to realize he had reached the first branch. He had been focusing so hard on his dwindling strength that he hadn't noticed he had been approaching his goal!

Supporting himself with his left hand and foot, he groped with his free hand to grab the branch. When he released the trunk, he dangled by one hand, then twisted sharply, kicked his legs, and seized the branch with his other hand, too. Pulling with the last of his strength, he almost shouted with relief when the branch was firmly beneath him.

He gasped for breath, then glanced below. A gossamer mist blocked his view of the soil, but he knew the drop was serious. He sighed. With his fingers back to normal and his belt on the ground, how was he going to climb back down?

Lewis continued his ascent. Mercifully, this part of the quest was easy. The branches grew so densely together that they formed something like a long flight of stairs. At the same time, among the oversize leaves, he thought he spied the occasional movement — it was so unnaturally quick he couldn't be sure. There was also a sticky goo everywhere — odourless and hard to rub from his skin. Above him, too, on the tree's far side, he was sure he could hear a high-pitched squeaking, though it might have been a trick of the wind. Not that it mattered. The weed was all that counted.

He climbed and climbed, whistling to himself, wondering how he would return to the soil. If he threw the weed down, assuming he found it, his friends would realize he was stuck in the boughs and maybe launch a rescue attempt. He also thought about his recent dream, the one in which guards had emerged from a pool. The dream seemed to be communicating something, but what?

There it was again, a high-pitched squeaking — *eek, eek, eek*. Who else was in the tree with him? And that goo was everywhere and sticking to his feet.

Without warning he gained the top. One moment

he was scrabbling from one branch to its neighbour; the next a network of branches parted, the mist thinned dramatically, and … his head was in the clouds!

How high was he? A mile perhaps, give or take a hundred yards. It was a good thing the mist blocked his view of the region. The sight of all that scarred and battered land would have weighed his spirits down even more. It was terrible how much misery men like Grumpel created!

A flash of yellow caught his eye. On his right there was a frail plant with a stark green base and bright yellow tips. The third ingredient! There it was! Scarcely able to believe this sight, Lewis plucked the plant and tucked it away as if it were the choicest of jewels.

"Now all I have to do," he said to himself, "is find a way to conquer gravity."

His elation quickly faded. How *would* he return? And even if he accomplished this trick, they had to find those twin crests, locate the lock, pick it open, and —

There it was again, that high-pitched sound, only louder this time and much more desperate. The noise told Lewis it was time to go. Ducking back into the leaves, he began his descent as quietly as possible, in case he wasn't alone.

"*Eek, eek, eek!*" The squeaking was off to his right.

"Keep going," he told himself, gathering speed. Unlike his upward climb, when the leaves parted freely, the tree now seemed to block his progress.

Over to his left had something moved? There had been a streak of brown against the leaves and something big and hairy. "You're imagining things!" he scolded himself.

"Eek, eek, eek!" The shrill sound persisted — it contained a note of panic, as if someone or something were pleading for help.

"I have problems of my own!" Lewis muttered, only to hesitate when the noise rang out again. It projected such sadness that he couldn't ignore it. With a heavy sigh he veered to his right. As he did, a flash of brown intruded and he passed yet another puddle of goo.

"All right! I'm coming!" he yelled, even as he wondered if this sound were a ploy and that some creature was luring him into a trap. Debating whether the risk was worth taking, he spied the squeaking party ahead, a few yards past a thin screen of leaves.

On an outer branch a shape hung in a net. Its struggles were causing the net to tighten, and as the knots drew closer, the trapped creature grew more desperate, thrashing about with whatever strength it still had. Curious, Lewis inched forward.

There. He could see it. He was faced with … a bat! Like every other beast in that region, it was larger than normal and roughly his size. Its back was furry and matted with oil, and its wings, while folded, were detectable still — they looked like giant sheets of leather. Catching wind of his presence, the bat met his eye.

Lewis almost laughed. The face was like a giant mouse's — friendly, frightened, and non-aggressive. Its eyes reflected intelligence, too. In fact, the creature's expression seemed almost human. Lewis crouched beside the bat and addressed it softly, even though he knew they couldn't understand each other. The bat, in turn, nuzzled his hand.

"What have we here?" Lewis asked, giving the net a quick going-over. Its strands were made from the goo he had spotted earlier and had been fitted to the branch to form a snare. What nut would have climbed so high to lay such a trap?

"It doesn't matter," Lewis said, assessing the strands. "Our main goal is to set you free. It's a good thing I'm handy with knots, because this trap is ingenious. Incidentally, my name is Lewis."

"Eek," the bat answered more calmly.

"The central knot is here," Lewis said, pointing at a tangle above the bat. "And it'll loosen once I've slackened these six outer ones." He set to work on the knots, humming to himself as the bat watched him closely. "That's five of them. There's just one more and the main one will slip."

"Eek," the bat commented, studying Lewis's fingers.

"I'm telling you," he repeated, handling knot number six, "whoever set this trap is a master, though I wonder —"

"Eeeek!" the bat screeched, staring past Lewis's shoulder. The hairs on his neck stood up. He glanced around slowly and almost dropped off the branch.

He should have known. A *web*, not a net, entangled the bat. And its creator was poised a few feet away, at the start of the branch where it joined with the trunk.

Normally, Lewis was fond of spiders. When he caught one in his room, he always carried it outside. They were no bigger than an inch, however, unlike the monster confronting him now. Its abdomen and thorax were two feet across, while each leg was more than a yard in length.

Its body was a light, poisonous brown, with hundreds of bristling hairs on its surface, like a porcupine's quills, only deadlier-looking. A pair of fangs pointed straight at Lewis — they were oozing venom. Worse by far were the spider's eyes: there were eight of them of varying sizes. Black and intelligent, they twitched simultaneously as they studied him.

"Easy there," Lewis croaked, snaking his hand around a nearby twig — it was dry and stout and would break off easily. The bat was nibbling at the sixth and final knot.

Even as Lewis traded stares with the spider, there was a rush of motion and a crowd of babies joined their mother. They were a tenth her size, but their fangs meant business. Their eyes, too, jiggled like crazy as they sized up their victims for a taste of meat.

Lewis snapped the twig off with one twist of his hands. "Stay back!" he warned, twirling his weapon.

For a moment the babies seemed to obey, but then two leaped forward, front legs raised. The bat, meanwhile, kept chewing the knot.

Lewis stamped his foot. "I said keep back!"

The mother flinched and drew her legs together, but the babies out in front kept edging toward him.

Lashing out, Lewis kicked the first off the tree — it was like striking a loose collection of rags. Then he knocked the other with his club and crushed its thorax. "We're in a jam!" he told the bat as the spiders began hissing. Lewis glanced at the bat and determined that it was halfway through the knot. He wanted to tell it to chew more quickly, but a movement signalled they were under attack.

A dozen babies were rushing him at once. Half were on a high branch and closing in from above, while the others were moving in from below. The mother, for her part, was sidling toward him, all eight eyes focused on his club.

Pff, pff, pff. He knocked three off the tree, two others were crushed, and a sixth was impaled. As it writhed on his staff, the mother lunged forward. *Pff, pff,* it lost two eyes. One leg missed him by a matter of inches.

"Hurry!" Lewis screamed. "I can't hold them off much longer!"

There was another rush and another. One spider reached his knee before he struck it with his fist, and twice he was bitten, but his outfit held firm. The bat, too, was almost overwhelmed. Five spiders tried to swarm it, but Lewis beat them back.

He was tiring. The climb, and now this battle, had him just about beat. His arms were heavy and his chest heaved. The spiders sensed it. They were massing together, above and below, and the mother was sidling in for the kill.

"This is it!" Lewis gasped.

One landed on his head and scratched his scalp with its bristles. He lurched and tossed it into space, only to feel his club slip away.

It was the mother. With a hiss she threw his club behind her and eyed him tauntingly as he raised his fists. A moment later she pressed against him, together with her babies, who were advancing in a swarm. Two legs thrust him against the bat, her six eyes fixed him with a hungry stare, and her fangs reached for his jugular.

Four babies were on his shoulders and three were on his knees. There was a smell of something rotting — the stink of death perhaps. He closed his eyes and waited for the fangs to strike.

"Eek!" he dimly heard from behind. There was a whirl of black and the babies went flying. The mother, too, was pitched into the air. *"Eek!"* the bat repeated, now free of the web.

Lewis glanced around. The mother spider was hanging by a thread and climbing furiously toward the branch. Her babies, too, still had plenty of fight. Calmly, the bat arranged Lewis on its shoulders.

The mother had returned and was steaming toward them. The bat squeaked again — it sounded like a laugh — and leaped into the encompassing mist. The pair dropped like a stone for a second until the bat spread its wings and braked their descent. Fast as a bullet, it circled the tree — the spider and her babies were watching in fury — then down it swooped to the soil with breathtaking ease.

Although Lewis was reeling from his exchange with the spiders, he knew he had won himself a friend for life.

CHAPTER 16

The bat ferried him to the ground so quickly that Lewis could hardly believe he was out of harm's way. A minute earlier he had been battling spiders; now he was together with his friends again. They were relieved to see him in one piece and slapped his back and ruffled his hair. The bat, too, nuzzled him all over.

"Thank goodness you're back," Adelaide cried. "We were beginning to suspect something awful had happened."

"The steel on your fingers is gone," Alfonse said as the frogs sprayed a rock with their food transformers.

"And look at your clothes," the Stranger clucked, motioning to rips the spiders had inflicted.

"Who's your friend?" Todrus asked with a good-natured smile.

As everyone sat and snacked on the goop, Lewis described the events in the tree, mentioning the weed and how the bat and he had wrestled the spiders. Even as he spoke, the bat pitched in. The Stranger listened closely — the translation brew was still inside it — and moments later turned the bat's speech into English.

"He's very grateful. If not for you, he would have been torn to pieces. Incidentally, his name's Atara."

They were all greatly taken with the bat. Lewis asked, via the Stranger, how his new friend had wound up getting stuck in the web.

"The mist threw him off," the Stranger revealed, listening closely to the bat's rapid cheeping. "By accident he flew into the Forbidden Region. When he realized where he was, he fell into a panic, started flying blindly, and crashed into that web."

"What's the Forbidden Region?" Lewis asked.

"It's what the bats call Yellow Swamp," the Stranger translated. "They're forbidden to go there because the place is so spooky."

"Spooky?" The group stopped eating and looked at one another.

"The place is haunted," the Stranger explained. "Not a single creature lives on its shores, yet the bats detect a presence, something different and … deadly. That tree was bad, but the swamp is even worse."

"So what are his plans?" Lewis asked, deeming it wise to change the subject.

"He would love to stay and chat," the Stranger replied, "but his family must be frantic about him. If you don't mind, he'd like to go home."

Lewis stared into Atara's eyes. The Stranger didn't have to translate for them. They were thanking each other from the bottom of their hearts and expressing the hope that they would meet again in the future.

Squeezing Lewis and cheeping farewell, Atara barrelled into the air. They watched him closely as he circled the oak, then vanished into the mist.

"We've been thinking," Todrus said, handing Lewis

back his belt, "about the situation."

"Oh?"

"He means the Alienus," Adelaide explained. "For once my brother said something of interest."

"In *Bombardier 19*," Alfonse pitched in, "Dr. Gong breeds dinosaurs in the Arctic and changes the climate to one the dinosaurs can live in."

"That story got me thinking," Adelaide went on, "how Alienus might need a special place to take shape in."

"The right sort of temperature," Todrus added, "or the right mix of moisture and soil conditions."

"You're saying Yellow Swamp was changed so Alienus could grow in it?" Lewis asked, focusing his eyes on the tree trunk. It explained a lot. Most chemicals only formed if their surroundings were perfect — the air and soil as Todrus had suggested. But why not create these conditions in a lab? And why install a lock when Grumpel's guards could watch over the substance? And why stash it far away in northern Alberta?

Lewis was about to raise these questions when a movement caught his eye. He sat up straight and squinted hard. Above the ground, at the beginning of the mist, a spider was gingerly descending the trunk. It was too far off to tell exactly, but it looked even bigger than the mother he had battled.

"Which way to the swamp?" he asked, reaching for his shoes.

"It's that way," the Stranger replied, pointing to a stretch of rock.

"Then let's get moving!" His shoe straps tightened, he jumped to his feet.

"What's the rush?" Adelaide asked. "Why not rest?"

"There's no time," Lewis cried, securing his belt. "A spider's climbing down and others will follow. We'd better go."

"There's a second one, too," the Stranger said. "They're both gigantic."

"Then what are we waiting for?" the Pangettis demanded. Although they seldom agreed on anything, both hated spiders with a passion. As soon as Lewis hurried off, they dashed behind him, with the frogs and Stranger bringing up the rear.

The going was rough. The stones underfoot were coated with moss and slippery as ice in a number of places. Here and there a boulder intruded, and when it couldn't be skirted, it had to be climbed. The worst part was the path's incline. Its thirty-degree slant was hard on the calves and had them all fighting to catch their breath.

They pushed themselves for a good thirty minutes. At one point the path became noticeably steeper, then, at the end of that stretch, it ended abruptly. If Todrus hadn't been on hand to grab him, Lewis would have pitched into space.

"Oooh!" the group cried, staring into a void. This mountain face wasn't at all like the one they had climbed to escape the murderous forest. Whereas the first had been rather easy to scale, this one presented a vertical drop and rock that betrayed no handholds or ledges. One slip, one misstep and ... goodbye forever.

Lewis surveyed the landscape below. It consisted of a barren plain whose earth was charred and dotted with craters as if it had been the stage for a serious battle. Beyond this blighted and empty expanse, which extended for at least fifteen miles, was yet another sea of fog — smoky white and vaporous. It ran on to the edge of the horizon, and for a moment it brought the Pother to mind, though it didn't seem as unforgiving.

The group retreated several feet from the edge.

"Yellow Swamp is beyond that fog," the Stranger announced.

"That's just our luck," Alfonse said bitterly. "Our destination is straight ahead, yet the face here is impassable."

"It certainly is," Gibiwink agreed. He was dizzy just from looking over the cliff.

"It could be worse," Todrus commented. "We'll return to the easy side, make our way down, then circle the mountain."

"That's not an option," Lewis said tersely. "We have to climb here."

"He's right. Look!" Adelaide yelled, her face ashen.

They glanced back. Three hundred yards away, and advancing quickly, was a wave — no, an ocean — of spiders. They easily numbered in the thousands and thousands. Although these arachnids were still a distance off, it was clear that some of them were truly monstrous, much larger than the one Lewis had fought in the tree.

Everyone's mouth hung open in shock.

"What should we do?" Gibiwink whimpered.

"How can we escape an army like that?" Alfonse murmured, trying to control his shaking hands.

To increase the travellers' panic, the spiders were producing a nerve-shattering sound. It was like the hissing of the mother spider Lewis had fought in the tree — only a million times louder.

The one piece of luck was that these spiders were slow. With the exception of the ones Lewis had battled earlier, these creatures had been hibernating half an hour before. Robbed of her prey, the mother had clambered about the tree and roused her neighbours from their deep winter sleep. That meant these new spiders were still a bit woozy.

"You have to delay them!" Lewis cried. He was flipping through his manual in search of some suggestion: *frost, fulcrum, fumes, funeral, fungus, fur, jeans, jet, justice ...*

"Leave it to us!" Todrus called, shaking off his fear. As the others gathered a pile of stones to throw at the spiders when they came within range, the frogs busied themselves with the boulders. Straining against a rock the size of a car, they managed to roll it toward their attackers. Because they were standing on a steep incline, bit by bit the stone gained momentum until it smashed into the spiders like a speeding train.

Lewis looked up briefly. He saw the boulder squash the enemy's front line, leaving legs and goo all over. As everyone cheered, the spiders replenished their ranks, hissed even louder, and beat their legs against the soil, creating such a wall of sound that Lewis and his friends were almost knocked off balance.

"They're yelling 'Fresh food!'" the Stranger warned.

"Keep stalling them!" Lewis cried, his nose in his manual: *machete, masquerade, matches, mattress, medicine, melting ...*

The frogs rolled another five boulders forward, and again smashed dozens of spiders to pieces — their blood was actually blue in colour. Unfortunately, their ranks were so tightly packed that the stones didn't slow their progress even slightly. If anything, their determination grew, because the fresh spring air and their mounting rage were awakening them from their winter torpor. Two hundred yards yawned between them and their victims.

The Stranger started hurling stones. Every missile found a target and sheared off legs and knocked out eyes, but the army kept advancing, even the wounded among them.

Moisture, mould, mulching, oil, ointment, old age, oscillation ...

Eight more boulders crashed into the arachnids' ranks. The stones, too, were flying thick and fast. Despite their many casualties, the spiders didn't pause and betrayed no sign of fear or hesitation. They were now one hundred and fifty yards off and collectively formed an impenetrable wall. The larger ones were noticeable now — they were thirty feet high, with legs so long and hairy that they looked like girders on a half-finished building.

Paddles, pain, paint, pants, parachute, pasteurized, patience ...

"A parachute!" Lewis yelled as the spiders doubled their pace. "I think I've found an answer! Hold them back three more minutes!"

"You heard him!" Todrus called. He and Gibiwink dislodged another boulder that rolled a hundred yards and crashed into a spider colossus. Four of its legs were mashed into pulp, and the creature toppled onto the spiders around it — like a tower landing on a crowd below.

And still the masses advanced.

Lewis and Adelaide set to work. They poured twelve drops of adrenyalienanitrate on a boulder, as well as a handful of polyalienaplebiscite, and topped the mixture off with ten milligrams of chalalienappendicitis. As the stone's hard surface began to bubble, they climbed on top and jumped up and down, smiling as the rock gradually flattened.

"They're eighty yards away!" Todrus cried.

"Keep stalling them!" Lewis yelled.

Alfonse mixed several fire grenades — he had no fear of attracting flies given the spiders' presence. As soon as he finished counting to thirty, the others hurled them into the throng. *Kaboom! Kaboom!* The effect was impressive. Dozens of the creatures were reduced to cinders as a wall of fire filled the air.

The flames soon died and the masses kept advancing.

"Hurry, Lewis! We're running out of tricks!"

Lewis and Adelaide kept pummelling the stone. By now it was as flat and supple as a blanket. It was twenty feet long and twenty feet wide.

"They're really close!" Alfonse cried.

"One minute more!" Lewis shouted.

Three grenades exploded, while the frogs heaved another five boulders. Again lots of spiders died, but the effect was tiny. Some smaller ones were skipping ahead, intent on getting a taste of meat. Todrus and Gibiwink smashed them flat with their flippers, but not without getting bitten in turn.

The hordes were thirty yards off. The hairs on the

big ones were visible now — they were three feet long and strong as steel.

"We can't hold them!" Todrus moaned.

"Grab hold of the parachute!" Lewis shouted, pointing to a sheet the size of a lawn.

The group retreated to the cloth. As the spiders hissed, stamped their legs, and lumbered forward with their fangs upraised, the friends reached the parachute and lifted it together. It was feather-light — never mind its "base" had weighed a few tons — but hanging on proved difficult. A breeze filled its hollows and pulled hard on the fabric, almost yanking it from everyone's grasp. It also dragged them to the edge of the cliff.

Five drooling spiders were ten yards away.

"Form a belt!" Lewis cried, shaping a strap from the fabric. Without wasting a second he tied it around his waist.

"They're about to strike!" Alfonse yelled.

"Do as Lewis says!" Todrus croaked, strapping himself in.

The others followed suit. By now the lead spiders were eight feet away. Seven. Five. Three. Two. One.

"Jump!" Lewis ordered.

A dozen spiders lunged. They snapped their legs and flailed their legs, but a gust grabbed the cloth and swept the group to safety.

Except they plummeted a hundred feet.

"It's not working!" Gibiwink screamed.

"It will!" Lewis shouted.

"I'd rather crash," Adelaide cried, "than be eaten by spiders!"

But neither fate awaited them. Bit by bit the chute filled with air, and bit by bit their velocity slowed. When they were roughly halfway to the ground, an updraft caught them and they started to rise. Within seconds they were nearing the crest again.

A line of spiders was waiting. Some were scaling the mountain face, hoping the wind would blow the chute into their clutches.

"Gibiwink! Todrus!" Lewis called. "Try tugging on your end of the cloth! That should steer us away from the cliff!"

The frogs yanked hard on the cloth. Sure enough, the chute veered off from the mountain. The spiders hissed and stamped their legs in fury. Moments later they had faded from sight and there was nothing but a grey pall above and a plain of blackened craters below.

They were headed toward the fog in the distance, with a temperate breeze to speed them on. No one spoke. They were too worn out for conversation.

The plain drifted by. It was a sobering sight. The craters looked like bullet holes, wounds the earth would never manage to heal. Again Lewis felt a twinge of conscience. It was because of his mother, and their trip to Yellow Swamp, that Grumpel had become aware of the region and altered it beyond recognition. If only she hadn't told him about its existence. If only she had refused to be part of his team. If only her wish to build an unbreakable lock hadn't clouded her judgment. If only …

They continued floating. With the mountain now a speck in the distance, the plain gradually ended and the fog took over. At the same time the wind began to wane, causing them to descend bit by bit until they were in the thick of the mist.

Gibiwink yawned. "This mist is nice. It's making me sleepy."

"Stay alert," Todrus warned. "We're getting close to the ground."

"Are we still on course?" Lewis asked, straining to see the land below.

"Dead on course," the Stranger said. "In fact —"

Before the Stranger could finish, the mist dissolved. Everyone gasped at the sight below.

They were hovering above a small lake, two miles wide and two miles long. The strange thing was that its water was red, exactly the colour of blood. Its consistency was a lot like jelly — when the wind touched its surface, it jiggled all over.

The weirdest part was the shape at its centre. It was a hundred feet long, some fifty feet high, and featured two mounds, one large and one small.

Before Lewis could speak, Gibiwink cut in. "Todrus, can you feel it? The place has changed, but we're finally home!"

"You mean ..." Adelaide started to ask.

The frog chuckled. "Yes! We've reached Yellow Swamp."

CHAPTER 17

As the group digested Gibiwink's announcement, the parachute carried them over the lake. Observing the hills and red water below, Lewis found the area unfamiliar. He couldn't believe his family had once camped there. At the same time he felt vaguely apprehensive. Never mind that they had attained their goal — as Atara had insisted, the place seemed … spooked.

"We have to reach those crests," Todrus said. "They're the ones Elizabeth Grumpel described."

"Let's steer toward them," Lewis agreed. "Adelaide, Alfonse, pull to your left."

The Pangettis pulled for all they were worth, and the parachute veered and approached the two hills. When it overshot their target, everyone yelled in panic — they were terrified they would end up in the blood-like liquid. Todrus pitched his weight to one side, while the Stranger chewed a hole in the fabric. Bit by bit the parachute drifted back until it floated above the larger crest.

There wasn't time to waste. Loosening their belts, they dropped onto the soil — it was rubbery and cushioned their fall. A moment later the parachute shot into the air and was soon just a tiny speck in the distance.

"Let's eat something," Lewis advised as soon as the parachute faded from sight. "And then we'll hunt for my mother's lock."

Everyone thought this was a good idea, and Alfonse sprayed the ground with his food transformer. But it was odd. Nothing happened. The spray had no effect.

"Your equipment must be broken," Adelaide said. "I'll use mine."

She sprayed the soil, as did Lewis and the frogs. The results were the same — the earth didn't change.

"What do we do now?" Gibiwink asked.

"Without these transformers we'll starve," Alfonse wailed. "It's like episode 31 when The Bombardier —"

He would have rambled on, despite his sister's frown, if the Stranger hadn't motioned them to silence. It was probing the soil and looked very concerned. "We're not standing on a hill. We're on something … alive."

"That's impossible!" the group exploded, "Nothing grows this big!"

"Whether you like it or not," the Stranger insisted, "this entire mountain is a living creature. Luckily, it's been thrown into a trance of some sort."

"How can you tell?" Alfonse finally asked. "These look like genuine hills to me."

"It's talking in its sleep," the Stranger explained, "and that translation brew is still inside me. It keeps muttering, 'Let me go, let me go, let me go.'"

"That's impossible!" everyone began again, but Lewis cut them off.

"I'm afraid it all makes sense," he declared. "The puzzle's been solved."

As the group turned their gaze on him, Lewis ran through what they knew already. Alienus came from a different planet. Grumpel used it in all his inventions, but his supplies were running thin. He did have more of the stuff on hand, only it wasn't quite "ripe" and had to develop — that explained why he had altered the Yellow Swamp region. This new climate would allow the substance to … hatch.

"So far so good," Alfonse said. "Now tell us something new."

"He just did," Adelaide insisted. "He used the word *hatch*."

"Do you remember," Lewis asked, facing the two frogs, "how you described Grumpel's destruction of this region? You said his henchmen dropped a stone into the swamp?"

"Yes, it was six feet high and shaped like an egg," Gibiwink said.

"Like an egg, exactly," Lewis confirmed.

Todrus looked aghast. "Wait! Are you —"

"Yes," Lewis continued, "the object was an egg. And it wasn't a meteorite that struck Grumpel's farm, but a creature just like this one here. It provided him with Alienus but, five years on, it's all used up. Lucky for him there was an egg left over, but it had to be hatched in the right surroundings, in an environment that would resemble the alien's planet. Obviously, he couldn't transform New York City — he would have called attention to his plans — so that's why he altered Yellow Swamp instead. Fewer people would notice in northern Alberta."

"And the lock?" Adelaide asked. "Why would Grumpel need —"

"He installed it," Lewis answered, "to hold the creature until it became full-grown. Now that it's an adult, he's ready to free it."

As they considered his words, and marvelled that an alien was lying beneath them, Lewis sized the creature up. What sort of lock could keep a mass like this in place?

"But wait," Alfonse said, "what will stop it from leaving once we've opened the lock? How can Grumpel —"

"Think about his guards," Lewis suggested.

Alfonse was confused. "His guards? How do they tie in?"

"I get it!" Adelaide cried. "The guards were wearing rings, remember, and that's how Grumpel is able to control them. He uses radio signals."

"There you go," Lewis said, leafing through his booklet. "I'll bet this alien's wearing a receiver, which will kick in the instant the lock is broken. In other words, it can't run off, but will return to Grumpel like a dog to its master. There!"

He tapped an entry in the index — *oxygen supply*. Before his friends could ask what he was up to, he selected four vials and tore a strip off his outfit. Using this fabric as a mixing base, he blended the chemicals and produced a sickly green concoction.

"But we have to free this creature," Gibiwink moaned. "How?"

"That's *my* concern," Lewis insisted, taking off his shoes and socks. He then removed the poem's ingredients and handed them to Todrus. "I want you to analyze these chemicals and find out what happens if you mix them."

"I … what … when …" Todrus stammered. Finally, he said, "I'll do my best."

"Try to find an answer by the time I get back."

"Get back?" the group demanded. "Where are you going?"

"I'm off to find the lock, of course."

"But where will you look?" Alfonse asked.

"Down there." Lewis motioned to the blood-red water. As the others told him he was out of his mind, he reminded them of Elizabeth's words — that they would find the lock at the base of these "hills." Saying that, he bolted the mixture down.

Almost instantly his tongue swelled up like a miniature balloon. Compressing it, he felt a jet of air shoot out, just as the entry in the book had predicted. He smiled at his friends — his oversize tongue made speaking difficult — then approached the creature's edge and jumped.

The next thing he knew the fluid had engulfed him. In was pleasantly warm and like jam in texture but lacked the buoyancy of normal water — it was only by pumping his arms and legs briskly that he could counteract its downward pull.

Luckily, the fluid was translucent. From above it had seemed dark and spooky, but the sky's dull light was passing straight through it. True, it wasn't perfectly clear, but it did let him see maybe ten feet ahead. And while water blackened the deeper one sank, this substance retained the same brightness throughout.

It was time to dive. Keeping the creature's flanks to his right — the thing was like an ocean liner — he folded his arms and sank ten feet, fifteen, twenty, twenty-five … He wondered how far it was to the bottom and, more important, how long his oxygen would last. The brew was amazing, though. By compressing his tongue every half-minute, he was able to keep his air supply steady.

Lewis continued sinking. Again unlike water, which got colder the deeper one dived, this fluid became hotter and hotter until he worried it might scald him. Its pressure also didn't change as he sank.

Without warning he struck bottom. A veil of mud spiralled around him, like ink being squirted from a fountain pen. Glancing up, he spied a trail of bubbles, one that climbed all the way to the surface. He also saw that the creature was vast. Lewis might have been standing at the foot of a castle the way its bulk towered above him.

What's keeping you in place? he mused as he travelled past its flanks.

Lewis walked around the creature, poking and prying and inspecting its surface. There wasn't any sign of a lock — no bars, no chains, no titanium walls. And if the Stranger hadn't told him otherwise, he would have sworn he was dealing with a rock formation. If it really was an alien, what was keeping it immobile? He glanced around in frustration, unsure what he was looking for.

Wait! The swamp's bottom was tilted downward. He swam off from the creature and held his face to the floor, working hard to churn his way through the fluid. Ten yards, fifty, a hundred he travelled. He was thinking he was searching for a needle in a haystack when he happened to stumble and …. aha! There was a hole of some kind!

It was round, wide, and six feet deep. It also marked the lowest part of the swamp. The ground surrounding it sloped slightly upward, like the porcelain around a bathtub drain. He dropped into the hole and landed ankle-deep in mud. Falling to his knees, he scraped the muck to one side. He toiled diligently until … a glint flashed out!

It turned out he was standing on a metal disk. It was the size of a sewer head and constructed from chronolium, a bluish-silver metal that was impossible to blast through. As Lewis stroked the disk, he felt a lump in his throat — he was kneeling on the last of his mother's achievements.

Lewis was about to examine the disk more closely, but suddenly his air wasn't flowing so well. The oxygen mix was starting to fail! Without wasting a second he shot toward the surface.

He had been under too long. Paddling frantically away from the bottom, he squeezed his tongue and produced a weak stream of air. How far was the surface? Sixty feet at least.

His limbs were like concrete. His lungs were on fire. Three times, four, he compressed his tongue and barely produced a mouthful of air. He was thrashing upward as hard as he could but was hardly able to prevent himself from sinking, let alone swim through fifty feet of "jam."

He paused for a moment to rest … and plunged fifteen feet.

That's it, he thought. *I'm as good as gone.*

He wasn't. A pair of arms grabbed him and propelled him upward as if he had hitched a ride on a speeding submarine. He squeezed his tongue in desperation. Not the slightest bit of air was produced. *Help! Hurry!* He was starting to shake. Five more seconds and his chest would explode!

He broke the surface with a terrific splash. Gobs of oxygen filled his lungs, sweet as sugar, more precious than gold.

"Aruhokay?" Gibiwink asked, clutching him still. The frog's speech and bulging cheeks revealed that he had swallowed some of the oxygen brew.

When Lewis nodded between deep gasps, Gibiwink explained he had jumped in after him because it was crazy for anyone to dive alone. A good thing, too. If he hadn't left that bubble trail behind …

"Thanks," Lewis said, tapping the frog. At the same time he began swimming to the "hills" where his friends were anxiously awaiting his return.

"U thood west," Gibiwink advised, swimming beside him. "U uhmotht died …"

"There isn't time to rest," Lewis panted. "I know the swamp's secret, except for one detail, and I'm hoping Todrus has pieced it together."

Again the frog propelled him forward. In no time at all they were nearing the creature — it was like pulling up to a ship at anchor — and Lewis asked for Todrus, after assuring everyone he was feeling okay.

"Hello!" Todrus hailed him. "Aren't you coming up?"

"No," Lewis answered. "Have you looked at those ingredients?"

"Yes. That blue stone contains an anabolic compound, while the flower, if its anhydrolic base is changed —"

"Thpeak in Englith!" Gibiwink yelled.

"The ingredients can be mixed to form a powerful acid. It won't do anything to glass or skin but will eat through metal in a matter of seconds."

"Bingo!" Lewis cried in triumph. After praising Todrus for his expertise — the frog actually blushed with pleasure — he asked how long it would take to prepare the acid. When Todrus answered a mere five minutes, Lewis told him to go ahead and to place the acid in an empty vial. He then called on Adelaide to mix a large batch of the oxygen brew and to store it in a vial, as well. Without questioning his orders she set to work.

In the meantime the pair continued to float. As they waited, Lewis explained the situation to Gibiwink — how the swamp was like a tub with a chronolium plug, a metal that very few acids could melt through.

"So dat's wad de poem was descwibin'," Gibiwink said, his tongue gradually returning to normal. "A recipe for bweakin' up de cwonowium pwug?"

"Exactly," Lewis said.

"But why would Grumpeh biwld a giand dub?"

"Look at this creature. Grumpel knew your average lock would be useless against it, so he had my mother trap it in a chemical bath."

"U mean?"

"As long as the creature's in this fluid, it can't move or awaken or do anything violent. It's stuck, like a bike that's been chained to a fence."

"So if you destwoy dat pwug, de swamp will dwain away?"

"Yes, through a network of pipes just under the swamp. And with the fluid gone, the creature will awaken."

Gibiwink had another question — would they be able to escape before the alien broke free? — but Todrus hailed them from the "hill" just then.

"It's done!" he cried. "I've got the acid!"

"And the brew's ready, too," Adelaide added.

"Great!" Lewis said. "Now tell everyone to join us."

"Join you? Are you sure?"

"Yes, and hurry please!"

As the group organized things above, Lewis told Gibiwink why they had to jump. If they waited until the swamp was drained, there would be no water to cushion their fall. At the same time, with the fluid gone, the creature —

Splash! The Stranger landed nearby, Todrus followed, then the Pangettis appeared.

"Listen," Lewis declared after greeting his friends, "Gibiwink and Todrus will help me dive. The rest of you start swimming to shore. No matter what, you mustn't stop. *No matter what.* Do you understand?"

"But I want to help," Alfonse said.

"We do, too," the others insisted.

"We'll look after him," Todrus promised. "You three should get moving."

After a few more protests, the trio agreed. Handing Lewis the oxygen mix, Adelaide and the others started off. Because the shore was at least a mile away, they had their work cut out for them.

"Good luck!" everyone called to one another.

After allowing them a five-minute lead, Lewis asked the frogs to hold him steady. He then swallowed part of the oxygen mix and gagged a little as his tongue swelled up. The frogs followed suit. As soon as the brew kicked in, they began their dive.

Linking limbs, they plummeted like cannonballs. A minute later they were on the bottom and poised before the base of the creature. At Lewis's prompting the frogs swam close to the floor, disturbing its mud with thrusts from their flippers, and in no time at all they arrived at the "drain."

Lewis dropped into the hole. His aim was to clear the mud from the disk so that the acid could be applied to its chronolium surface. The frogs helped out by reaching into the drain, flailing their flippers and dispelling the grime.

There it was.

Even in that blood-red fluid the chronolium gleamed with hypnotic beauty. It looked strong enough to absorb a nuclear blast. Lewis sighed and stroked the plug again, amazed that his mother had built such a system.

Todrus pointed at his mouth — a warning that their air might fail. Lewis nodded and produced the vial, whose syrupy contents seemed … disappointing. How could it dissolve a solid layer of chronolium? Full of doubt, he held the vial near the plug, turned it upside down, and removed the stopper. When the paste oozed out, he assumed it would break up in the fluid, but it settled in a clump on the metal's brilliant finish.

Ten seconds passed. Nothing happened. Lewis fanned his hand to spread the paste more evenly, but it remained in a clump and triggered no reaction.

Thirty seconds passed. Had they been wrong about the poem? Had it been a bit of nonsense verse, with no bearing whatsoever on his mother's locking system? If so, how would they destroy this disk, assuming he was right and it really was a plug? Unless it wasn't and he had been wrong all along ...

He gasped as the frogs yanked him out of the hole.

The chronolium was blistering in front of their eyes. Its blue-silver length was now a pale yellow, and a blanket of heat engulfed the trio, as if the door to a roaring furnace had been opened. Flames were breaking out inside the fluid. While Lewis was afraid, he was also ashamed. He shouldn't have doubted his mother's instructions.

Grabbing Lewis, the frogs took off. They covered twenty yards in a matter of seconds and increased their distance with every stroke, but the acid's heat was spreading quickly. The fluid was bubbling wildly now.

But the heat didn't concern them that much. Their real fear stemmed from the plug's disappearance. As soon as it melted, the fluid would drain and they would be drawn toward the hole and sucked inside.

They were now three hundred yards from the drain and breaking through the water's surface. The fluid wasn't nearly so hot. Had they managed to escape its downward pull?

The three swimmers didn't have time to see what hit them. One moment they were pressing forward, the next there was a sucking sound and the entire swamp was spinning like crazy — as if they were trapped in an enormous blender.

"De pwug!" Todrus gasped. "De athid mus ha ea'en thwew!"

Before Lewis could answer, the swamp's spiral yanked him back. The frogs still clutched him, their legs kicking furiously as they battled the current. As hard as they fought, the torrent was stronger — not only were they sliding back, but the fluid was heating up again.

Oof! They struck the creature, and it was like hitting a brick wall. The collision winded Gibiwink and Todrus, and they briefly relaxed their grip on Lewis. Instantly, the current jerked him back.

Lewis was dragged across the alien's surface and would have shot into the whirlpool and been sucked into the drain had his hands not grazed a slight outcropping. He managed to latch on to it and took in his surroundings. Over there, on his right, was he imagining things? No, there really was a cave close by.

It was a fold in the creature's skin that could possibly shelter the trio.

"Todwus! Gib'wink! Ovew hewe!" he shouted. "I'b found a cabe!"

As the frogs glanced up, he waved them over. He also clasped the ledge with his feet, thereby freeing both hands. A moment later Todrus floated near, steering himself with the last of his strength. Hauling on his flippers, Lewis dragged him to safety.

"Get Gib'wink!" Todrus sputtered.

Gibiwink drifted near, as well, but was short of Lewis by a couple of feet. Any moment now and he would be swept away …

"Yaw tongue!" Lewis yelled. "Wap it wound me!"

Gibiwink obeyed. Catching hold of his tongue Lewis reeled him in and dropped him next to Todrus as if he were landing an unusually large fish.

For the next few minutes they huddled in the cave and listened to the fluid roar around them. They were worried about the rest of the group and whether their comrades had been able to escape the current.

"Am I cwazy," Gibiwink asked, "or is it wess noisy?"

"Yaw wight," Todrus said, rearing his head. "It *is* wess noisy."

They peered outside and were taken aback. The swamp's level had fallen and it was still draining. As more of it vanished, more of the creature could be seen. Below them was a long slope of grey, as if they were standing on a mountain of clay.

A gurgling erupted. The last of the fluid was running off, and the swamp's muddy bottom was visible in places. Here and there, where bits of silt had washed away, lengths of metal piping were exposed. But the best sight by far was the figures in the distance. Gibiwink waved. Their friends waved back.

The mud was now completely exposed. Strange to say, Lewis felt a bit bad because the absence of water marked the death of Yellow Swamp. At the same time, eyeing the soil below, he knew they had to act if they were going to survive.

"We've got to jump," he announced, his voice back to normal. "We're in danger here." Without awaiting their response he launched himself forward.

The creature's flanks were like a playground slide.

Because its skin was smooth and moist from the swamp, the long ride down was safe and easy. For a good ten seconds he continued to drop, gathering speed as he barrelled downward. Near the bottom the flank curled up a little, and when Lewis reached it hurtling at thirty miles per hour, it tossed him twenty feet into the air. Luckily, his fall was cushioned by a large patch of mud.

"Hurry up!" he cried. "There's no time to spare!"

"What's the big hurry?" Gibiwink grumbled. Todrus pushed him forward and followed swiftly behind.

"Are you okay?" Lewis asked some thirty seconds later, smiling at the frogs' mud-covered features. As they started to answer, his eyes widened in horror.

He had seen strange sights since they had entered the region, but the scene that now confronted him was the strangest yet by far.

"I think we have a problem," Lewis whispered to his friends.

CHAPTER 18

Everyone's mouths were open in shock. The creature before them had unfolded itself and was astounding. It looked a bit like a brontosaurus, only it had two crests instead of one and at least thirty legs, while a dozen wings sprouted out of its back, each the size of a helicopter's rotor. Its head alone was as big as a car, with a mouth large enough to swallow a human.

Near the top of its skull was a band of shifting colours that pulsed and crackled with electricity. And covering its flanks were hundreds of eyes, each full of fire and incessantly blinking, as if it were trying to signal its neighbours.

Lewis was transfixed — with wonder more than fear. There it was in front of him, proof that there was life on other planets, beasts as complex as the ones on Earth. Despite his worries he felt microscopic. Grumpel, Yellow Swamp, even his dad's captivity, these were all unimportant when compared to the universe's size and majesty.

The alien lifted its gargantuan head, opened its mouth, and produced an outlandish sound — a cross between a rumbling diesel engine and a bagpipe's howl. Then it gazed at the sky and unfurled its wings like a plane waiting for a runway to clear. Lewis wanted to examine the creature more closely, but for some odd reason his waist was burning …

It was his chemical belt! When the beast uttered its unearthly scream, the noise had caused all the vials to shatter in his belt and in the frogs', as well. Of course, the chemicals were mixing together.

"Get rid of your belts!" Todrus yelled, untying his and hurling it away. The others quickly followed suit. Sure enough, seconds later the belts exploded in a shower of sparks. There was a smell of rubber, plastic, and metal, and a molasses-like smoke filled the air. Then, quick as it flash, it all disappeared. A mile away there were two more explosions as Alfonse and Adelaide also dumped their belts — or so Lewis hoped. Unfortunately, the disturbance drew the creature's attention, and it suddenly swayed its head toward them.

"Run! It's going to kill you!" the others shouted from afar.

The frogs started fleeing, but Lewis stood his ground. Escaping this beast was out of the question; it made better sense to confront the alien directly.

The head passed within an inch of Lewis, and his body was reflected in the bands on its skull. Then he realized the image was more like an X-ray scan — his bones and organs were on display. The creature was analyzing him to see if he were tasty or posed a threat to itself. When it decided he was neither, it raised its head and shrieked again.

As Lewis pressed his hands to his ears, he noticed something shiny on the alien's neck — a foam or plastic patch of some kind. This had to be the receiver, he thought, and was Grumpel's means of controlling the beast. Before he could get a better look, the creature balanced on its hindmost legs — each was as thick as the trunk of an oak. At the same time it stretched its multiple wings and tautened its muscles the length of its body.

"It's going to take off!" Todrus shouted from a few yards off.

As the trio watched in fascination, the alien hefted itself and took to the sky.

It was hard to believe such a mass could fly, yet it not only climbed with breathtaking speed but wheeled in circles with the grace of an eagle a good three miles above their heads.

"What's it doing?" Gibiwink asked.

"It's catching its bearings," Lewis said, straining his eyes to keep the creature in focus. "There's a receiver on its neck, but Grumpel's signal must be weak."

His mind was racing. If this creature returned to New York City without them, Grumpel wouldn't feel obliged to free his father. In other words, they had to pursue it. But how? Before he had freed the alien, he hadn't known about its wings. He had also assumed that, if the going got rough, their belts would help them in any jam. But their belts were gone, the creature was airborne, and any moment it would return to the chemist.

Lewis closed his eyes. How could he fail after all their scrapes and near brushes with death? Yet short of sprouting wings, they couldn't follow …

As if in answer to his prayers, there was a distant cheeping. A formation was flying in from the plain, exactly like a line of jets. All at once it split itself in two — half headed toward the frogs and Lewis, while the rest approached the Stranger and the Pangettis.

It was Atara. Hearing the alien's shriek — the sound had carried for miles — the bat had thought his friends were in danger. Despite his fear of the Forbidden Region, he had gathered all his relatives and had come to the rescue. Lewis felt as if his heart might burst.

There wasn't time for lengthy greetings, though. The bat seated Lewis on his back and flew off at a dizzying speed. Within seconds Yellow Swamp was a mile below, looking more forlorn than ever without the beast at its centre. In the meantime Lewis's comrades had saddled their own bats and were shooting off after the creature, as well.

The alien was several miles ahead of them. Its wingspan was incredible, so observing it was easy. And though it was fast, the bats kept up.

"Atara says hello," the Stranger said, pulling alongside Lewis on a grey-speckled bat — Atara's uncle, as it turned out. "He says they'll carry you wherever you want."

Lewis laughed. "Tell him I can't thank him enough. But warn him that we're off to New York City. Can he and his relatives take us that far?"

"He says," the Stranger answered after a pause, "they'll carry you to the ends of the world until their hearts stop beating."

They were crossing a critical boundary just then. Until now they had been flying in the Yellow Swamp region, with its haze of grey forever veiling the heavens. Without warning the dullness ended and the sun was on their shoulders.

It was setting, and the sky ahead was purple. They were back in a world where normal rules applied, where boulders didn't explode, reptiles didn't speak, and lakes were filled with clear, plain water. In short, the Alberta landscape was a sight for sore eyes.

"It's so beautiful ... the sun!" Adelaide gushed.

"I could tackle that alien on my own!" Alfonse whooped.

"And Grumpel had better watch out!" Todrus added.

Grumpel. His father. New York City. Lewis gazed at the creature ahead and pondered what they would do when it reached its destination. Despite his gladness to see the sun, the hardest task lay ahead of them still, and success was far from certain.

His worries enveloped him, and he fell asleep.

Lewis was walking down a corridor. The walls were lined with newspaper clippings. Ahead of him were two chained doors — behind them he could hear the splash of water — only the padlock was gone and they were starting to open. Someone called, "Lewis! Lewis!"

Before he could answer, however, three armed figures burst out. "Don't shoot!" he yelled. "I'm here for my father!"

The figures only laughed and bore down on their triggers.

Lewis awoke with a start. The sky was black and there was silence. For a moment he couldn't place where he was until he felt Atara's wings beating beside him. Feeling Lewis stir, the bat began cheeping.

The Stranger yawned. "He says we've been asleep a long time. And we're also getting close to the city."

By now the rest of the group was awake. Gazing ahead of them, they gasped and sat up straight. They were still twenty miles off, but the lights of New York City were impossible to miss. The illumination sprawled across the landscape like an enormous glowworm, soft and welcoming and full of possibilities. Strange to say, the city seemed vulnerable as the alien sped toward its centre, obedient to Grumpel's beck and call.

But where was the creature? Lewis scanned the darkness but couldn't make much out. As he grew anxious, Atara cheeped beneath him.

"He says not to worry," the Stranger said. "He's tracking our target."

"How? It's way too dark to see."

"He's using sonar," Adelaide said. "He's tracking it by sound, not sight."

"That's right," the Stranger agreed.

"Eeek!" Atara added.

Lewis squeezed the bat in thanks. They were now soaring above the city's suburbs, passing cars and trucks and a slow-moving train. It was late at night, to judge by the traffic, and people were getting ready for bed. If they had known an alien was passing overhead, they might have been less … lackadaisical.

A pang of dread struck Lewis. It was *his* fault the beast was visiting the city, and if buildings were damaged or people got killed, there would be no one else to blame except him. Sensing this serious turn in Lewis's thoughts — bats were good at reading people — Atara wriggled and signalled his encouragement.

The next hour would end this adventure, for better

or worse.

They streaked over water — the Hudson River. As bright and lively as the suburbs had been, they were nothing compared to the brilliance that now engulfed them. The creature and bats had been gradually descending, and by now they were just a thousand feet above the ground. Tower upon tower rose to embrace them, and the storefronts, streetlamps, and headlights on the streets, not to mention lights from the various buildings, had them all blinking and rubbing their eyes.

Then there was an explosion of signs below — they were over Times Square. A snake of people exited a theatre. In the patrons' anxiety to hail a cab, they failed to notice the "invaders."

The travellers' bats grazed the Empire State Building. On its observation deck Lewis spied a guard with a metal flask in his hand. When the man looked up, their glances intersected. The guard's jaw dropped, and he tossed his flask away, convinced the alcohol was making him woozy.

They were following Broadway. The Flatiron Building passed in a flash, as well as Greenwich Village and Washington Square. Off to their left was the Brooklyn Bridge. Over to their right Ground Zero gaped, the site of the former World Trade Center, a hole in the city waiting to be filled. Ahead were Wall Street and the New York Stock Exchange.

"It's over by the river," the Stranger said, translating the bats' excited cheeping.

"We're nearing Grumpel's headquarters," Lewis said, "but how's he going to hide the alien's presence from the city?"

"We'll find out in a moment," the Stranger told him. "We're preparing to land."

The next thirty seconds passed in a blur. The bats were flying at breakneck speed, weaving between wires, billboards, and a thousand other obstacles. The bats' passengers held on with all their strength.

Lewis almost hooted — it was like riding the wildest of roller coasters. Near the tip of Manhattan, above Battery Park, he and the others had to shield their eyes as a carpet of lights flashed on without warning.

The lights were set up on a warehouse roof, one that spanned three city blocks and that Lewis quickly recognized. They had left from here days earlier, though it seemed like years since they had last been in the city. In their absence the roof had been transformed. Besides the lights, huge panels had been erected that were high above the neighbouring buildings and concealed the roof's activities from them. Its surface was crammed with uniformed workers and a line of miniature cranes. Over in a corner was a two-man helicopter. In the centre of the roof was a huge yellow *G*, which it was clear the alien was preparing to land on. It slowly lowered itself toward the roof, its wings fanning the air with such force that its backdraft caused the tarpaulins to wobble and almost tore a row of lights from their mountings.

Grumpel and Elizabeth were present. They stood on a platform that would give them a view of the creature's tail when it landed. The chemist held a device equipped with dials, buttons, and antennae. He watched as the beast flapped its wings one last time and touched down on the roof with its legs outstretched. A moment later it folded its wings, drew its head to its body, and didn't move a muscle. Astonishingly, it again resembled a huge mound of earth.

"Now what?" Todrus asked as the bats hovered above this scene.

"We'll land and talk to Grumpel," Lewis said.

"You don't think we should try to ruin his plans?"

"Not until he releases my father."

"But will he keep his promise?" Adelaide asked.

"If he doesn't free my father, we'll think of something else. In the meantime ..."

Lewis tapped Atara. The bat plunged to the roof, with his family behind, and Lewis felt his stomach leap into his head. A moment later they braked within an inch of the roof's surface. Lewis and his friends quickly dismounted in view of Grumpel and the army of henchmen. Before the guards could lift a finger, the bats barrelled off and settled on the panels thirty storeys above the proceedings. From here they could watch how matters developed.

Until then the guards had been scurrying about and readying things for the creature's landing. With the group's appearance the bustle stopped. Grumpel himself was stunned, and the guards were taking their cue from him. For his part Lewis was steadying himself — he had been straddling Atara so long that his legs were stiff and wobbly.

"Look who's here," Elizabeth sneered, fingering a Petriglobe gun.

"Welcome!" Grumpel announced. "And congratulations on a job well done. I have to admit, I didn't think you'd make it back."

"Well, we did," Lewis said with his hands on his hips. "And now that we're here, free my father like you promised."

Grumpel stared at him, then broke into laughter. It had been twelve years since he had cracked a smile, and another five since he had laughed outright. That explained why his chuckling had such a ghastly ring. "This is better than I'd hoped," he wheezed. "It just so happens I'll need a good locksmith in future, and that's why our arrangement is going to continue. In other words, you Castormans aren't going anywhere!"

He motioned to a knot of workers wheeling a machine toward the creature's tail. The device was equipped with a hose and nozzle attached to an oversize receptacle. It was exactly like a vacuum cleaner, only it was large enough to handle a fully grown adult.

"That wasn't the deal!" Lewis cried hotly. "You said you'd free my father!"

"This isn't fair!" the others also yelled. "You promised!"

"Quiet!" Grumpel roared. "I'll do as I please!"

He signalled to a second group of workers. They approached the creature with a ladder in hand and a tool that looked like a circular saw. When the ladder was propped against the creature's tail, a pair of workers climbed to the topmost rungs, balancing the heavy saw between them. A moment later the saw was on — the engine was silent but its blade spun viciously.

Grumpel chuckled. "You have no idea how much power this alien will give me."

"We know all about the Alienus," Lewis spat.

"So you've figured it out, have you? Then you know I can bend the laws of chemistry to my will."

"And even conquer death," Elizabeth chortled.

Grumpel laughed again, a bit more maniacally this time. "That, too."

"In that case," Lewis argued, "you can afford to release my father."

Instead of replying, Grumpel signalled to the workers with the saw, who touched the spinning blade to the creature's tail. Instantly, it shrieked and stretched its head toward its rump — its neck was long enough to touch its rear with its snout — but Grumpel merely adjusted his controls. Forced to obey, the beast fell silent and nestled its head against its flank.

"You're hurting it!" the group cried out. "Leave it alone!"

Grumpel sniffed. The workers had cut more than halfway around the tail and had traced an arc that was oozing yellow gel. When they were four-fifths around the base of the rump, they switched the saw off at a sign from Grumpel and descended the ladder.

The creature rocked and groaned.

Elizabeth waved to a third group of workers. They were seated in four mini-cranes, which they backed up to the tail, maintaining an eight-foot interval from one another. At the top of each crane was a long metal chain, which the drivers strapped to the length of tail before them. Once the chains were fastened, Elizabeth blew a whistle. The cranes rolled forward, causing the tail to pivot and twist away from the body like a door being opened on a well-oiled hinge.

Again the alien reared its head as a hole was exposed at the start of its rump, a bleeding, gooey entrance that led straight into its vitals. With the flick of a switch Grumpel again stopped its squirming.

Lewis studied the beast. Despite its size and frightening appearance, he pitied it greatly. It was alone, in pain, and had no one to protect it from the scheming chemist.

"How awful," Adelaide clucked from behind.

"We're almost there," Grumpel announced, nodding at the team with the "vacuum cleaner." "You'll understand everything in just a minute."

The device was rolled to the creature's rear. Stationing the machine at the start of its wound, two guards thrust the nozzle inside and explored its hollows. The alien was trembling so hard that the roof was shaking.

"What do they think it's hiding?" Alfonse whispered.

"Not *it*," Adelaide gasped, "but *she*. They're looking for —"

"Eggs!" Lewis cried.

"That's right," Grumpel called from above. "This wretched beast has eggs inside her, and *that's* the source of the Alienus. Better yet, I can plant more eggs in future and never have to worry that my supply will run out."

"And that's where I come in," Lewis said bitterly.

"That's where you come in," Grumpel agreed. "You'll repair your mother's lock for me and open it again when yet another 'chick' is grown."

"We've got one, sir," one of the guards with the nozzle announced. Lewis saw a silver orb emerge — it was six feet high and oval. The nozzle was about to suck it up.

"Careful, you idiots!" Elizabeth cried. "We want that egg intact, remember!"

The creature sensed her eggs were being stolen. She turned toward her gaping wound and moaned. Lewis felt sick with guilt. He desperately wanted to help the creature, to deliver her from Grumpel, but they were powerless.

Or were they? As the beast writhed in agony, he spied the patch on her neck — the receiver that was channelling Grumpel's signals to her brain. If the receiver was removed, the crazy chemist couldn't control her, and the creature would be able to escape her captors. All he had to do was …

"Todrus, Gibiwink," he murmured to the frogs, "can you keep this crowd of salamanders busy? Especially the pair with the vacuum cleaner?"

"Let us at them!" the frogs replied, hating to see the creature mistreated.

"What about us?" Alfonse muttered. "I'm dying to teach those goons a lesson."

"Do whatever you can," Lewis said. "Just wait for my signal."

Grumpel was pushing buttons again and forcing the creature to shy away from her wound. Her head was pointing forward and lay a hundred feet from Lewis. The guards, too, were back at work and about to suck the egg up with the nozzle. Grumpel and Elizabeth were eyeing them closely. In other words, it was now or never.

"Go!" Lewis rasped, sprinting to the half-severed tail.

There was a flurry of action. The frogs attacked the workers with the nozzle, while the Stranger and the Pangettis stormed the drivers on the cranes. For his part Lewis jumped onto the tail and climbed toward the creature's back.

"What are you up to?" Grumpel yelled. "You can't possibly stop — hey! Hands off my extraction unit!"

He was screaming at the frogs. Not only had they knocked several salamanders senseless, but Todrus had pushed the nozzle aside, while Gibiwink was rolling the egg into the creature, careful not to crack the shell.

Alfonse's group controlled three cranes.

"Attack them!" Grumpel shouted.

"With pleasure!" his daughter snarled, sliding down the platform and nodding to some guards, all of whom were armed with Petriglobe rifles.

Lewis had reached the top of the creature's tail, which ended abruptly at the start of her rump. There was a gap in front of him and a hideous drop — he might have been poised on the ledge of a building. Focusing all his energy, he jumped. He didn't quite make it to the other side but managed to latch onto the top of her backside. After dangling for several seconds, he pulled himself up.

He glanced down. The Pangettis were spinning the cranes in circles and bowling crowds of salamanders over. And the Stranger was ramming guards by the dozen.

Plop. A yellow cloud erupted — it was a Petriglobe. Charging forward, he mounted the first crest and barrelled down its far side at breakneck speed.

Plop! Plop! Two salamanders had him in their sights. One Petriglobe fell wide, while the other grazed — and froze — his ear. Heavy thuds rang out, and the firing stopped.

"Keep going!" Todrus yelled, with the marksmen lying unconscious before him.

Lewis rushed the second mound. He was panting heavily, and his legs were numb. He kept ducking, too, to avoid being hit. Ten feet to the top, five, three, one. There, he had cleared it. All he had to do was ... No! In front of him stood a welcoming committee.

"Hello, boyo," the limousine driver called out at the head of a dozen guards. They had climbed the front of the creature to head him off. "Nice of yuhs tuh make it. Stick 'em up!"

Lewis balled his fists in frustration. Behind the salamanders was the alien's neck and, more important, the patch he was after.

"I said stick 'em up!" the driver growled. With no choice in the matter Lewis slowly raised his arms.

The bats appeared with the fury of a whirlwind. One moment Lewis was in the line of fire, the next the salamanders had been knocked out cold. *Biff, biff, boff,* the path was clear.

The patch. Lewis ran five paces and pitched himself forward.

Time seemed to slow. Petriglobes were exploding everywhere — Elizabeth's crew was firing from below. Lewis was the intended target, but the bats caught the pellets and were frozen in his place. For his part, Lewis went hurtling through the air until he wound up colliding with the creature's neck. Because its neck was satin smooth, he began sliding earthward and scrabbled madly to brake his fall. At the very last moment his nails caught hold of something. His fingers were nearly yanked from his palms, but he held on to the edge of this surface.

He was hanging from the lip of the receiver!

Six feet long and six feet wide, it was soft to the touch and felt like skin. That made sense, he realized quickly, because this patch had expanded as the creature had grown. The material, too, was very strong. It wasn't much thicker than a piece of cardboard, yet was managing to hold Lewis aloft. It had been glued to the creature's side, however, and the adhesive was weakening beneath his weight. With a few brisk tugs …

"Well, well, what have we here?"

Elizabeth! She was standing in front of a crowd of henchmen some fifteen yards below. While some were pointing their rifles at Lewis, others were guarding the rest of the group. Alfonse's and Adelaide's hands were raised, four guards were pinning the frogs' flippers behind them, and the Stranger's tentacles were confined to its sides. And the bats were scattered all over the place, frozen in shells of orange, pink, and yellow.

The patch was starting to peel away from the creature.

"Get a ladder!" Adelaide cried. "Before he falls and hurts himself!"

"We'll save him," Elizabeth sneered, "as soon as he agrees to work for us."

"I'll never join you!" Lewis yelled. He swung his legs wildly to help the patch along. Six inches of it were dangling loose.

"Only an idiot doesn't know when he's been beaten!" she cried.

"Better an idiot than a thug!" Lewis gasped. A foot of the patch had peeled itself free.

"I'll give you one more chance!" she said. "Are you with us or against us?"

"I'd rather be dead than work for you!" Lewis retorted, using the last of his strength to loosen the patch further.

"Have it your way!" Elizabeth shrugged, lifted her rifle, and squeezed the trigger.

Several things happened at once: Adelaide and the others screamed; Atara, who had been lying in wait, flew beside Lewis and intercepted the pellet; and the patch came away all at once, so that Lewis and Atara plunged earthward together. While the bat landed on a knot of henchmen, Lewis struck Elizabeth, who crumpled beneath him.

"Get that boy!" Grumpel roared. "Riddle him with Petriglobes!"

The guards closed in, but Lewis ignored them. He was kneeling beside Atara, who was frozen in a case of yellow. "I'm so sorry," he murmured. "As for you," he said, facing the chemist, "you may think you've accomplished a lot, but you're really just a cold-blooded killer! From now on no one's going to talk about your talents. Instead they'll remember just how lousy you were and will curse your memory forever and ever."

"Freeze him!" Grumpel ordered his guards.

The guards were about to pull their triggers, but it was exactly then that the alien stirred. She had shifted her weight several times already, but this movement was different ... less restrained. With the receiver gone Grumpel couldn't issue her orders, and she was waking up to this fact. Twisting backward, she inspected the crowd — Grumpel on his platform, the salamander guards, Elizabeth, who was standing again, and Lewis, who was tending to Atara.

Grumpel was the first to recover, worried that his schemes were about to collapse.

"Don't just stand there!" he bellowed at his henchmen. "Capture those eggs before the creature flies off! And the rest of you, forget the intruders and hold this creature back until the eggs are clear!"

"You heard him!" Elizabeth cried. "Open fire on this brute!" She retrieved her rifle, aimed at the alien, and squeezed off several volleys.

The guards did the same, firing pellets at the alien's flanks. At the same time the extraction unit crew moved in and shoved the nozzle deep into the egg sac.

Lewis was going to attack Elizabeth, while the frogs were preparing to battle the guards. But there was no need. The creature herself was part Alienus, and the Petriglobes proved useless against her. With a single kick she scattered her attackers, then bent her neck toward her tail and grabbed the extraction unit with her lips. With one quick flick she tossed the machine out to sea — it landed near a freighter and soaked a sailor on deck.

Lewis was about to cheer. Before he could get a sound out, however, the creature brought its "rainbow" band to his face. There he was, reflected in its waves, dancing lines of yellow, orange, and purple. It was impossible to tell what the creature was thinking, and for a moment Lewis thought she would crush him like an insect. Just as swiftly he sensed in her a wisdom that predated human thinking and understood that she hated violence through and through. The sooner she went home, the happier she would feel.

"Go," he murmured. "The way is clear."

As if responding to his words, she rose on her hindmost legs, spread her wings, and lifted off.

"No!" Grumpel shrieked as the alien departed, her wings creating such a powerful draft that for a moment everyone was pinned to the spot. Lewis watched as she soared a hundred feet, then gasped as an egg suddenly fell toward them. It turned out her wound had closed, but not before one egg had slipped free.

With a heave of her sinews, the creature vanished. A second later there was a soft explosion and, almost immediately, a blue powder filled the air, covering Lewis and everyone around him.

"Gather up that dust!" the chemist cried, clambering down the platform three steps at a time. "Hurry, you fools! Each teaspoon's worth a billionaire's ransom!"

It was useless. As much as his workers scrambled about, the powder was too delicate to trap. It melted before their eyes and sank into the roof. At the same time — or was it Lewis's fancy? — the salamanders began shrinking and grew confused.

"Trap it! Hold it!" Grumpel hollered, chasing a blue spiral until the wind broke it up. Elizabeth was pursuing the powder, too, but apart from the dust that had settled on her outfit, she wasn't faring any better than her father. The sight of them spinning in circles like that caused Lewis and his friends to howl with laughter.

"So much for your plans!" Todrus jeered, rubbing his stomach where he had been struck with a rifle. His head was covered with so much powder that he might have been dipped in a pot of blue paint.

"I have my army!" Grumpel snarled. "Kill them, guards! Do you hear? Attack!"

They couldn't. Grumpel had been chasing the powder so intently that he hadn't noticed the change it had triggered. Each henchman that the substance had touched — and it had spattered every guard on the roof — was changing back to its normal appearance. From tall, intelligent, and capable of speech, they were shrinking to their usual size and losing all signs of their mental adeptness. In fact, mere minutes after the egg had exploded, every guard was a simple reptile again, and outfits and metal rings lay scattered at random.

Grumpel's army was no more.

"You're finished!" Lewis cried as salamanders scurried in a crowd from the roof. "You're out of chemicals and your army's gone."

"I may have lost, but you haven't won!" Grumpel roared, racing to the helicopter in the roof's far corner. "Elizabeth, quickly!"

As fast as everyone moved to stop them, father and daughter reached the helicopter first. A moment later the propeller was turning and they were hovering ten feet in the air.

"Say goodbye to your father!" Grumpel snarled over a speaker. "If my tale ends badly, yours will, too!"

Before Lewis could reply, the helicopter barrelled off to the west, its blades spitting insults into his ears.

CHAPTER 19

Lewis wanted to yell at the helicopter, but he had other, more pressing concerns. The egg's blue powder was changing everything. Besides transforming Grumpel's army, it was seeping into the building's foundation and reducing it to a jelly-like substance. From one end to the other the roof was shaking, and the towering panels were glowing all over.

"We've got to leave!" Todrus cried.

"How?" Adelaide demanded. "The roof isn't solid!"

"This is like The Bombardier's battle with the Slime," Alfonse said as everyone sank to their knees in jelly. By now the building had lost much of its shape.

"I hear sirens," Gibiwink said. "Help is on its way!"

"It had better come soon," the Stranger advised, "because this building isn't going to last much longer!"

Lewis wanted to kick himself. So Grumpel had won. The chemist had lost the Alienus and his empire was in ruins — the powder was "jellifying" his underground towers. On the other hand, Lewis's father would die and the group would drown in this liquefied stone.

"Eek!" something cheeped from on high.

"Atara?" he asked hopefully.

The bat was suddenly hovering above him, along

with all his relatives. They were bruised, bedraggled, and covered in powder, but alive and kicking nonetheless.

"Raise your arms!" the Stranger called. "They'll help us track that chopper down!"

"How did they escape?" Alfonse asked. "Weren't they frozen?"

"It's the powder!" Todrus cried. "It's neutralizing everything — the guards, the Petriglobes, the underground towers. It's a nucleonic inhibitor that —"

"Will it affect us, too?" Gibiwink groaned.

"Never mind!" the Stranger insisted. "Lift your arms!"

The bats took action. One moment Lewis and his friends were on the verge of drowning, the next they were a hundred feet above the chaos. And as soon as they were airborne, Grumpel's building collapsed. Above ground and below it, the structure splattered apart, flooding the streets with "gooified" stone. As a line of fire trucks arrived at the scene, the "jelly" hardened to the earth it had been, obliterating every trace of Grumpel's fortress forever.

"What do we do now?" Alfonse asked, smiling at the sight of this ruin.

"The bats can't hear the chopper," the Stranger observed.

"It was flying west," Adelaide declared. "Maybe we'll spot it if we fly that way."

Everyone agreed. The bats headed west at an impressive speed but without their usual energy, as if an unseen force were holding them back. And what was true of them was true of the others. The frogs looked worn and the Stranger was fading — its tentacles were drooping and its eye had swollen over.

Lewis felt awful. He wanted to give his friends a rest, but he had to track his father down. They might be headed in the right direction, but Grumpel had a huge head start, and if he reached his father first, he would kill him for sure. Where was he? Where? There were a million possibilities, and they didn't have time —

"In episode 9, The Bombardier's after the Mould," Alfonse told them, clueing into Lewis's thoughts. "He finally finds him in an obvious spot."

"So?" Adelaide snapped.

"So we're heading west," Alfonse continued, "and Grumpel owns businesses in Mason Springs. Maybe he's hiding Mr. Castorman in one of them."

"That's … that's … smart," she conceded. "If I were him, I'd keep my prisoner close by."

"So we'll fly to Mason Springs," Todrus said, "and search those businesses. *Ugh!*"

"Todrus! What's wrong?" Gibiwink cried.

"It's nothing," his friend whispered. grimacing. "Just a cramp from all that exercise."

The bats by now had crossed the Hudson River, and the lights of New Jersey lay directly below. They were flying at four hundred miles per hour and would reach their destination soon. The only problem was that they were utterly spent. Their passengers were just too much for them.

"Eeek!" Atara's uncle said — he was moaning that his wings were about to drop off.

"Eeek, eeek!" Atara replied. That meant "We can't let

Lewis down!"

Even as Lewis was on the verge of despair, part of him burst with pride. He had friends who would risk their lives for him. Never mind his fancy cars, Grumpel didn't have any companions like these and that meant he would never be as rich as Lewis.

A familiar sight dispelled these thoughts. It was 4:00 a.m., and the streets were empty, but Lewis recognized his town straightaway. They were directly over the central strip, and below them Grumpel's Bank appeared, as well as Grumpel's Clothes and Books, and Food and Flowers, and Cars and Hardware — all the businesses the chemist owned.

"Look around!" Adelaide yelled. "We should see signs of the chopper!"

The bats made several sweeps, moving west a mile, then returning east, not just once but several times. There was no trace of Grumpel.

"The bats are finished," Alfonse said.

"The others are, too," Adelaide murmured.

It was true. The bats were trembling and panting with exertion, while the frogs and the Stranger were deathly pale. They had to land soon and let everyone rest.

"Eeek!" Atara whimpered, convinced the bats were disappointing Lewis.

With a smile Lewis stroked the bat's ears. He was about to steer him to the ground, in fact, when he caught sight of their school. Lewis sat up straight as his dream returned, the one that had haunted him on several occasions, about the trophy case and doors to the pool and gunmen and …

"That's it!" he yelled, startling the others. "Atara, one last favour. Can you set us down by that building over there?"

"He says he can," the Stranger answered, even as the bats veered ninety degrees.

"But that's our school!" Alfonse cried. "Why —"

"It's the perfect hiding place," Lewis explained. "Its pool has been abandoned these past few years and no one would think of looking inside it. All along I knew there was something suspicious — its lock was rearranged the day we cleaned those letters — but I didn't put things together … until now."

"When we last saw your dad," Adelaide said thoughtfully, "he was seated below his guards and water was dripping — just what you'd expect if he were trapped in a pool."

She might have added more if the bats hadn't faltered. They were landing on the school's front lawn, but this feat was just too much for them. One by one they fainted away, upsetting their passengers and pitching them forward. The Pangettis wound up in a tangle of bushes, while Lewis collided against the trunk of an oak. By the time the group recovered from their tumble, the bats were gone.

"Where —" Lewis started to ask.

"Look! You were right!" Todrus shouted, motioning to a shape beneath a green tarpaulin. "Grumpel's helicopter."

"We have to get inside!" Lewis insisted, his thoughts returning to his father. He hurried to a door and fumbled for his picks.

Todrus coughed, heaving his bulk into action. "Let me." Although he was unsteady and wheezing like a bagpipe, he approached the letters that spelled the name of the school. With a twist of his flipper he pried the *G* in *Grumpel* loose. Then he took careful aim.

"Now *this* I'm going to enjoy," Alfonse gloated.

There was a crash. Lewis and Alfonse couldn't help but smile as a window smashed into a million pieces.

"Todrus?" Gibiwink asked, clutching his friend. The frog was swaying and clutching his head.

"Never mind me. Let's rescue Mr. Castorman!"

Lewis climbed the windowsill and passed inside. The others followed in his wake, though the frogs and the Stranger needed assistance.

There was a half-open door at the room's far end, and light was entering from the hall outside. Lewis exchanged nods with Alfonse. They were in their classroom — Ms. Widget's ruler lay across a desk beside a stack of compositions. Lewis tiptoed to the door. Glancing around, he motioned the group into the hall and led them toward the school's main foyer. Only half the ceiling lights were on and the place was unfamiliar in the gloom. Portraits of Grumpel hung on the walls, and his eyes seemed to watch them as they stumbled forward.

They reached the hallway's end. Turning right, they heard a disturbance in the distance. There. Past the cases with the chemist's trophies, past the clippings, photos, and seven-foot statue, the Grumpels were huddled by the pool's twin doors. There was a third party with them. Winbag, of course.

The school principal was dressed in a pair of lemon-lime pajamas that called attention to his strange dimensions. He was missing a slipper, and his glasses were absent. This last detail was important — without them he couldn't see which key would open the lock.

"Hurry!" Grumpel yelled. "I've been waiting five minutes!"

"My humblest apologies," the principal crooned. "I've forgotten which key belongs to this lock. Just one more minute —"

"In another minute you'll be fired!" Elizabeth growled.

"Right you are. And may I say, Miss Elizabeth, you look most fetching."

"Can it and get that lock unfastened!"

"All right. There. *Now* we're getting somewhere."

Winbag had slipped the proper key into the lock, but the pins were rusty and it wouldn't pop open. At the same time Todrus had a coughing fit, and the sound attracted the trio's attention. Grumpel's mouth dropped open in horror. For once in his life he was badly outnumbered. Hiding behind Winbag, he took hold of the key.

The principal examined the newcomers. From friendly and ingratiating, his expression had hardened. "You!" he roared, glaring at Lewis. "What are you doing here?"

"Your boss is about to kill Lewis's father," Alfonse snarled.

"Wait!" Winbag fumed, ignoring Alfonse. "The doors are locked. How did you get in?"

"We broke a window," Adelaide answered. "To rescue Mr. Castorman."

"Broke a window?" Winbag squealed. "That's flagrant vandalism!" Behind him Grumpel sniggered as the lock snapped open. Elizabeth began unwinding the chain.

"Step aside," Lewis said. "There's no time to explain."

"What? You dare?" Winbag's face was fire-engine red. His hands outstretched, he rushed at Lewis. Before he could touch him, the frogs interfered and hurled the principal the length of the foyer. He crashed into the trophy case where a large gold-plated chemical beaker — the Carston J. Plugman Award — bonked him on the skull and knocked him senseless. Just in time, too, as the doors wheeled open.

"After them!" Lewis thundered, charging forward and jamming his foot in the door. On the door's far side stood three hulking guards — they were the last of Grumpel's army. Determined to bar their passage, these goons strained at the doors, while Lewis and his friends tried to shove them open. Normally, the frogs could have handled the job, but their strength was failing.

"Push!" Lewis screamed, eyeing Grumpel through a crack. He was twenty feet away with two vials in his hands. One contained its stopper still, but he was emptying the other into the pool at his feet. "Use all your strength! He's killing my father!"

There were gobs of powder on Gibiwink's flippers. He held one to his mouth and blew its dust at the henchmen. With a shriek they retreated, and the group burst in.

It was much like any room with a pool — fifty yards long and ten yards wide, with tiles underfoot and a cathedral-like ceiling. The space hadn't been dusted in ages, however, and the only light was coming from the pool itself, from the lamps that ran the length of its sides. The effect was eerie.

"Stay where you are!" Grumpel warned. He was several yards away at the edge of the pool. He looked … murderous. His eyes and forehead were cast in shadow, and his expression was mocking, hard, and vicious. In one hand he held an empty vial; in the other he clutched a tube with a pale, pinkish substance — a deadly mixture, to be sure. Elizabeth was beside him, glowering like a wolf.

"What have you done?" Lewis yelled, not daring to attack. He was too far back to see the pool's bottom, but assumed his dad was below Grumpel.

"It's not what I've done," the chemist sneered, "but what I'm going to do. This first brew melted the Petriglobe's membrane, while *this* one …" He shook the pinkish brew. "One drop will change your father forever!"

"Let him go!" the frogs and the Stranger mumbled. They meant this as a threat, but it sounded … insubstantial. The three of them were trying to hold on to the guards.

"Lewis? Is that you?" another voice broke in, frail but recognizable still.

"Dad!" Lewis cried, taking one step forward. "Watch it! Grumpel's about to hit you with some poison!"

"That's right, Castorman!" Grumpel spat. "And there's nothing you or your brat can do about it!"

"Zap him, Dad!" Elizabeth shouted. "It'll serve them right for ruining our plans!"

"No!" Lewis screamed, charging the chemist.

Events unfolded in slow motion: Lewis rushed Grumpel, though he was too far off; the chemist laughed as he tipped the vial; and Gibiwink leaped forward and struck the vial with his tongue. Even as he hit its glass, there was a puff of smoke and the group was enveloped in a thick haze.

Time snapped back to normal. For a moment there was an unnatural stillness. The vial lay in pieces on the tiles, the puff of smoke had disappeared, and everyone's shrieks had faded to silence. Lewis hardly dared to study the scene.

"Holy smoke!" Alfonse whispered.

"What is it?" Adelaide gasped.

The Grumpels had been struck, not Lewis's father. Where the pair had been standing was the ugliest sight imaginable. Twitchy, awkward, and semi-transparent, like enormous bacteria, they lay there and studied each other. A hole then opened in each of these monstrosities and Lewis heard a revolting sound — it was a squeak, belch, and whistle combined. The chemist and his daughter were screaming in horror.

"Thissss issssn't over," the larger one gurgled. "We'lll be back!"

"We'll crush you, Lewissss Cassssstorman," the second one hissed.

The two figures slithered into the pool and oozed across its tiles to the drain in its middle. With a ghastly, slurping, slippery sound, they contorted themselves and spiralled downward to wind up in the city's sewage system.

Even as their squelching faded, a shadow stirred on the floor below. A hand appeared, a mane of hair, then finally Mr. Castorman was visible. A moment later he was embracing his son. For the next few minutes no one said a word, but stood there in a ring, unable to believe this happy ending.

"I'm so proud of you," Lewis's father finally whispered. "I don't know how you did it, but you've defeated a powerful and dangerous man."

"The Pangettis helped," Lewis said, pointing at his friends. "And so did Todrus, I mean, Mr. Todfrey, and Mrs. — wait! Where is everyone?"

He glanced around the room, and his spirits deflated. Seated on two uniforms was a pair of wood frogs — frail, lethargic, and back to normal. Beside them three salamanders were looking around with dazed expressions.

"Todrus! Gibiwink!" Lewis cried. "What happened? Where —"

"It's the Alienus," Adelaide said tearfully. "It got all over them and changed them back — and that's what happened to the bats outside."

"They can't just leave!" Lewis said. "I mean, Grumpel's been beaten ..."

"I'm so sorry ..." his father started to say when another, distant voice spoke up.

"Lewis?" someone whispered by the exit. The voice was scratchy but somehow familiar.

"This ... this isn't possible," Alfonse stammered when he spotted the "intruder."

"My brother's right!" Adelaide gasped, her eyes

wide with fear. "How can this be? You're supposed to be ... dead!"

Lewis and his father turned together. Both of their jaws dropped in shock. Before them, in a diving mask and air tank, was Lewis's mother, Sarah Castorman!

CHAPTER 20

Lewis was thrilled, delighted, overwhelmed, flabber-gasted, and disbelieving when he saw his mother standing in the pool room. Before he could get out a word, however, a hundred police officers and firefighters burst in. The police were holding guns at the ready, while the firefighters had extinguishers and axes in hand.

Winbag had alerted them when he regained con-sciousness. Because the principal had sounded frantic, with his talk of giant frogs and a freak with tentacles, an emergency response team had rushed to the school. Apart from broken glass and a few wandering reptiles, they could see that everything was under control.

"So what's the big emergency?" the police chief demanded, striding to the head of the crowd. He scowled when a frog climbed onto his shoe. By the markings on its skull, Lewis knew it was Todrus. "Let me guess," he continued. "An aquarium broke and your pets got loose."

Laughter erupted. The police officers tucked their guns away and the firefighters set their equipment down. Some of them started stroking the frogs. They were surprised when the amphibians showed no fear of humans. One cop grinned when his nose got zapped — that was Gibiwink's doing.

"You don't understand!" Winbag yelled from the doorway. He had refused to enter, convinced there were monsters inside. "They were here just a minute ago. Ask Mr. Grumpel himself."

"Is that so?" the police chief said. "Where *is* Mr. Grumpel?"

As Winbag searched for his boss, Lewis knew it was time to speak up. "Mr. Grumpel left, with his daughter in tow. They were in a big hurry."

"Who are you?" the police chief asked. "And why are you here at 5:00 a.m.?"

Lewis exchanged looks with his friends. He could reveal the truth about the alien, Yellow Swamp, the giant spiders, and his mother's miraculous return, or he could tell a more believable story. He glanced at the police chief. The man seemed kind but very practical. When Alfonse shook his head, and his parents did the same, he knew exactly what to say.

"Well, sir, my friend and I are always late for school — our principal will tell you so himself. This morning we decided to show up early, together with my parents and Alfonse's sister."

"What about the window and the broken case?"

"I think they were Mr. Grumpel's doing. He was performing an experiment, and it caused an explosion."

"And these animals?" The chief almost smiled as Todrus ducked inside his jacket.

"They're part of our family," Lewis said. "We bring them everywhere."

"And what about your diving outfit?" the chief asked Mrs. Castorman.

"I was hoping to test it in this pool," she answered, "only to discover that Mr. Grumpel hasn't filled it."

"I see," the chief said, suspecting there was more to the tale. "I suppose that explains everything."

"Wait!" Winbag insisted. "What about those creatures I mentioned? And something tells me Mr. Grumpel's in danger. Don't listen to this pack of lies! I'm a principal, and he's ... he's —"

"He's a smart and gutsy kid," a voice broke in. Everyone jumped as a figure approached. Lewis recognized him straightway.

"Fire Marshal Stephens," the police chief said. "I didn't notice you in all this commotion. You can vouch for this boy and these people with him?"

"You bet I can," the fire marshal said, standing next to Lewis and shaking his hand. "He's the most competent locksmith I've ever laid eyes on. The gutsiest one, as well," he added, winking at the Castormans, who beamed with pride.

"He's a treasure," Mrs. Castorman agreed. "And we'd keep him under lock and key, but he'd pick his way past them."

"That settles that," the police chief concluded as soon as the crowd's laughter subsided. "But just so you know, it's Saturday and the school is closed. As for you," he said to Winbag, who was still muttering about damage to school property, "the next time you call, you'd better not be clowning around, otherwise I'll place you under arrest. And, incidentally, put some water in this pool!"

The firefighters and the police officers then trailed

out, followed by the Pangettis and the Castorman family, with Gibiwink and Todrus riding high on Lewis's shoulders.

"What now?" Lewis asked, cutting into his pancakes. The group was seated in the Pangettis' bakery. When Alfonse's parents learned that their children were back — Grumpel had told them they were away on some project — they had pulled out all the stops and had cooked a first-rate meal, one that featured every pastry on the menu, together with regular breakfast foods.

"What now?" Mrs. Castorman asked, picking up a syrup jug. "To begin with, I'll renew my driver's licence. I imagine it's expired since I disappeared."

"Seriously," Lewis said to his mother as he fed a chocolate muffin to the frogs. "Take it easy," he told Todrus and Gibiwink as they bolted the food. "There's plenty more where that came from."

"There's a Smith D-Module I have to inspect," Lewis's father said, motioning for the syrup. "It's a lock on a Ferris wheel in London, England."

"D-Module?" his wife repeated, passing him the syrup with a look of mischief. "I thought the C-Module was the newest prototype."

"The D-Module appeared late last fall." He tilted the jug, but nothing came out.

"Was it painful," Adelaide asked Mrs. Castorman, "when you underwent that transformation?"

Mrs. Castorman laughed as her husband fiddled with

the jug. "You can't open it that way. And, tell me, who designed the D-Module?"

"Squeeze the handle and push the lid," Lewis advised his father.

"Mark Figstorm, who else?" Mr. Castorman said to his wife as he followed Lewis's suggestion. The syrup gushed out and flooded the table. Instantly, the frogs jumped into the mess.

"Well done, Lewis," Mrs. Castorman said, beaming. "You saw that two pressure points were needed."

"The oldest trick in the book," her husband groaned.

"And to answer your question," Mrs. Castorman continued, "it felt as if I'd been wrapped in plastic and stuck inside an old iron pot."

"What's it like to forget your past?" Adelaide asked.

"The Bombardier loses his memory," Alfonse muttered, freeing his finger from Gibiwink's tongue, "but even so, he refuses to use his powers for evil."

"Not The Bombardier!" Adelaide groaned. Eyeing Lewis and the Castormans, however, and her parents bringing yet more pastry to the table, she playfully stuck her brother with a fork. "Maybe I'll give your comics a try."

"It's true what you say," Mrs. Castorman said. "The crucial memories remain locked inside, even when everything else has vanished. And no one, not even a first-rate locksmith, can open that lock and help herself to those treasures. Although I'd rather not repeat that experience again."

Alfonse frowned. "There's one point I don't get. Why did the powder change the henchmen so quickly, while Todrus and everyone else lasted an hour?"

"I suspect," Mr. Castorman said after pausing briefly to consider the question, "that Grumpel's henchmen didn't like their boss and had no reason to resist the transformation. Your friends, on the other hand —" he patted Todrus "— were so attached to you that they managed to endure until the very last minute. Loyalty like that is more precious than gold."

"But what happens now?" Lewis repeated. "I mean, what about Grumpel? What if he returns? What if he gets his hands on more powder and builds his empire all over again?"

"The future's hidden behind a lock so strong," Mr. Castorman said, eyeing his wife and son with contentment, "that there's no sense trying to pry it open. You're better off taking full advantage of the present."

Alfonse chuckled, then pointed at a platter his father had put on the table. "Especially when the present includes hot cinnamon buns."

The frogs leaped forward and scattered the pastries. As everyone laughed and gathered the buns, Lewis understood that, even if the future proved dangerous, his friends and parents would be there to help him through it.

As if to prove that point, Gibiwink zapped him with his tongue.